Agatha Christie

While the Light Lasts

Background notes by Tony Medawar

HARPER

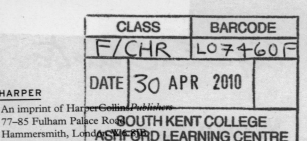
HARPER

An imprint of HarperCollins*Publishers*
77–85 Fulham Palace Road,
Hammersmith, London W6 8JB
www.harpercollins.co.uk

This *Agatha Christie Signature Edition* published 2003
7

First published in Great Britain by
HarperCollins*Publishers* 1997

Copyright © 1997 Agatha Christie Limited
(a Chorion company). All rights reserved.
www.agathachristie.com

ISBN 978-0-00-715485-2

Typeset by Palimpsest Book Production Limited,
Grangemouth, Stirlingshire

Printed and bound in Great Britain by
Clays Ltd, St Ives plc

Preface

Agatha Christie, the *original* Queen of Crime, still reigns supreme as the greatest and best known writer of the classical detective story. Her most famous novel, and very possibly the most famous of all detective stories, is *The Murder of Roger Ackroyd* (1926) in which she outraged the critics and, by doing so, established herself in the first rank of writers in the genre. That case was solved by Hercule Poirot, late of the Belgian Police Force, who appeared in 33 novels including *Murder on the Orient Express* (1930), *The ABC Murders* (1936), *Five Little Pigs* (1942), *After the Funeral* (1953), *Hallowe'en Party* (1969) and *Curtain: Poirot's Last Case* (1975). Christie's own favourite among her detectives was Miss Jane Marple, an elderly spinster who appeared in 12 novels, including *The Murder at the Vicarage* (1930), *The Body in the Library* (1942), *A Pocket Full of Rye* (1953), *A Caribbean Mystery* (1964)

Agatha Christie

and its sequel *Nemesis* (1971), and finally in *Sleeping Murder* (1976), which like *Curtain* had been written during the Blitz nearly 30 years earlier. And among the 21 novels that do not feature any of Christie's series detectives are *And Then There Were None* – originally published as *Ten Little Niggers* – (1939), in which there is no detective at all, *Crooked House* (1949), *Ordeal by Innocence* (1959), and *Endless Night* (1967).

In a career that lasted more than half a century, Christie wrote 66 novels, an autobiography, six 'Mary Westmacott' books, a memoir of her expedition to Syria, two books of poetry, another of poems and children's stories, more than a dozen stage and radio mysteries and around 150 short stories. This new collection brings together nine stories that, with a couple of exceptions, have not previously been reissued since their original publication (in some cases, 60 to 70 years ago). Poirot appears in two stories, 'The Mystery of the Baghdad Chest' and 'Christmas Adventure'. These are Christie's original versions of two novellas included in the collection *The Adventure of the Christmas Pudding* (1960). 'The Edge' is a tense psychological story and 'The Actress' involves a clever deception. The enigmatic 'Within a Wall' and 'The Lonely God' are romantic stories, dating from the earliest years of Christie's career; and there is a spice of the supernatural in 'The House of Dreams' and 'While the Light Lasts'. Finally, there is

'Manx Gold', a story whose form and concept was unique in its time but which has since become very popular all over the world.

Nine stories that all display the inimitable style of Agatha Christie. A true banquet for connoisseurs!

Tony Medawar
London
December 1996

Acknowledgements

With gratitude to John Curran, Jared Cade, Karl Pike, author of *Agatha Christie: The Collector's Guide*, and Geoff Bradley, editor of *Crime and Detective Stories*

T. M.

Contents

The House of Dreams

I

This is the story of John Segrave – of his life, which was unsatisfactory; of his love, which was unsatisfied; of his dreams, and of his death; and if in the two latter he found what was denied in the two former, then his life may, after all, be taken as a success. Who knows?

John Segrave came of a family which had been slowly going downhill for the last century. They had been landowners since the days of Elizabeth, but their last piece of property was sold. It was thought well that one of the sons at least should acquire the useful art of money making. It was an unconscious irony of Fate that John should be the one chosen.

With his strangely sensitive mouth, and the long dark blue slits of eyes that suggested an elf or a faun, something wild and of the woods, it was incongruous that he should be offered up, a sacrifice on the altar of Finance. The smell of the earth, the taste of the sea salt on one's lips, and the free sky above one's head – these were the things beloved by John Segrave, to which he was to bid farewell.

At the age of eighteen he became a junior clerk in a big business house. Seven years later he was still a clerk, not quite so junior, but with status otherwise unchanged. The faculty for 'getting on in the world' had been omitted from his make-up. He was punctual, industrious, plodding – a clerk and nothing but a clerk.

And yet he might have been – what? He could hardly answer that question himself, but he could not rid himself of the conviction that somewhere there was a life in which he could have – counted. There was power in him, swiftness of vision, a something of which his fellow toilers had never had a glimpse. They liked him. He was popular because of his air of careless friendship, and they never appreciated the fact that he barred them but by that same manner from any real intimacy.

The dream came to him suddenly. It was no childish fantasy growing and developing through the years. It came on a midsummer night, or rather early morning, and he woke from it tingling all over, striving to hold it to him as it fled, slipping from his clutch in the elusive way dreams have.

Desperately he clung to it. It must not go – it must

not – he must remember the house. It was *the* House, of course! The House he knew so well. Was it a real house, or did he merely know it in dreams? He didn't remember – but he certainly knew it – knew it very well.

The faint grey light of the early morning was stealing into the room. The stillness was extraordinary. At four-thirty a.m. London, weary London, found her brief instant of peace.

John Segrave lay quiet, wrapped in the joy, the exquisite wonder and beauty of his dream. How clever it had been of him to remember it! A dream flitted so quickly as a rule, ran past you just as with waking consciousness your clumsy fingers sought to stop and hold it. But he had been too quick for this dream! He had seized it as it was slipping swiftly by him.

It was really a most remarkable dream! There was the house and – his thoughts were brought up with a jerk, for when he came to think of it, he couldn't remember anything but the house. And suddenly, with a tinge of disappointment, he recognized that, after all, the house was quite strange to him. He hadn't even dreamed of it before.

It was a white house, standing on high ground. There were trees near it, blue hills in the distance, but its peculiar charm was independent of surroundings for (and this was the point, the climax of the dream) it was a beautiful, a strangely beautiful house. His pulses quickened as he remembered anew the strange beauty of the house.

The outside of it, of course, for he hadn't been inside. There had been no question of that – no question of it whatsoever.

Then, as the dingy outlines of his bed-sitting-room began to take shape in the growing light, he experienced the disillusion of the dreamer. Perhaps, after all, his dream hadn't been so very wonderful – or had the wonderful, the explanatory part, slipped past him, and laughed at his ineffectual clutching hands? A white house, standing on high ground – there wasn't much there to get excited about, surely? It was rather a big house, he remembered, with a lot of windows in it, and the blinds were all down, not because the people were away (he was sure of that), but because it was so early that no one was up yet.

Then he laughed at the absurdity of his imaginings, and remembered that he was to dine with Mr Wetterman that night.

II

Maisie Wetterman was Rudolf Wetterman's only daughter, and she had been accustomed all her life to having exactly what she wanted. Paying a visit to her father's office one day, she had noticed John Segrave. He had brought in some letters that her father had asked for. When he had departed again, she asked her father about him. Wetterman was communicative.

'One of Sir Edward Segrave's sons. Fine old family, but on its last legs. This boy will never set the Thames on fire. I like him all right, but there's nothing to him. No punch of any kind.'

Maisie was, perhaps, indifferent to punch. It was a quality valued more by her parent than herself. Anyway, a fortnight later she persuaded her father to ask John Segrave to dinner. It was an intimate dinner, herself and her father, John Segrave, and a girl friend who was staying with her.

The girl friend was moved to make a few remarks.

'On approval, I suppose, Maisie? Later, father will do it up in a nice little parcel and bring it home from the city as a present to his dear little daughter, duly bought and paid for.'

'Allegra! You are the limit.'

Allegra Kerr laughed.

17

'You do take fancies, you know, Maisie. I like that hat – I must have it! If hats, why not husbands?'

'Don't be absurd. I've hardly spoken to him yet.'

'No. But you've made up your mind,' said the other girl. 'What's the attraction, Maisie?'

'I don't know,' said Maisie Wetterman slowly. 'He's – different.'

'Different?'

'Yes. I can't explain. He's good looking, you know, in a queer sort of way, but it's not that. He's a way of not seeing you're there. Really, I don't believe he as much as glanced at me that day in father's office.'

Allegra laughed.

'That's an old trick. Rather an astute young man, I should say.'

'Allegra, you're hateful!'

'Cheer up, darling. Father will buy a woolly lamb for his little Maisiekins.'

'I don't want it to be like that.'

'Love with a capital L. Is that it?'

'Why shouldn't he fall in love with me?'

'No reason at all. I expect he will.'

Allegra smiled as she spoke, and let her glance sweep over the other. Maisie Wetterman was short – inclined to be plump – she had dark hair, well shingled and artistically waved. Her naturally good complexion was enhanced by the latest colours in powder and lipstick. She had a good mouth and teeth, dark eyes, rather small and twinkly, and a jaw and chin slightly on the heavy side. She was beautifully dressed.

'Yes,' said Allegra, finishing her scrutiny. 'I've no doubt he will. The whole effect is really very good, Maisie.'

Her friend looked at her doubtfully.

'I mean it,' said Allegra. 'I mean it – honour bright. But just supposing, for the sake of argument, that he shouldn't. Fall in love, I mean. Suppose his affection was to become sincere, but platonic. What then?'

'I may not like him at all when I know him better.'

'Quite so. On the other hand you may like him very much indeed. And in that latter case –'

Maisie shrugged her shoulders.

'I should hope I've too much pride –'

Allegra interrupted.

'Pride comes in handy for masking one's feelings – it doesn't stop you from feeling them.'

'Well,' said Maisie, flushed. 'I don't see why I shouldn't say it. I *am* a very good match. I mean – from his point of view, father's daughter and everything.'

'Partnership in the offing, et cetera,' said Allegra. 'Yes, Maisie. You're father's daughter, all right. I'm awfully pleased. I do like my friends to run true to type.'

The faint mockery of her tone made the other uneasy.

'You are hateful, Allegra.'

'But stimulating, darling. That's why you have me here. I'm a student of history, you know, and it always intrigued me why the court jester was permitted and encouraged. Now that I'm one myself, I see the point. It's rather a good rôle, you see, I had to do something. There was I, proud and penniless like the heroine of a novelette, well born and badly educated. *"What to do, girl? God wot," saith she*. The poor relation type of girl, all willingness to do without a fire in her room and content to do odd jobs and "help dear Cousin So-and-So", I observed to be at a premium. Nobody really wants her – except those people who can't keep their servants, and they treat her like a galley slave.

'So I became the court fool. Insolence, plain speaking, a dash of wit now and again (not too much lest I should have to live up to it), and behind it all, a very shrewd observation of human nature. People rather like being told how horrible they really are. That's why they flock to popular preachers. It's been a great success. I'm always overwhelmed with invitations. I can live on my friends with the greatest ease, and I'm careful to make no pretence of gratitude.'

'There's no one quite like you, Allegra. You don't mind in the least what you say.'

'That's where you're wrong. I mind very much – I take care and thought about the matter. My seeming outspokenness is always calculated. I've got to be careful. This job has got to carry me on to old age.'

'Why not marry? I know heaps of people have asked you.'

Allegra's face grew suddenly hard.

'I can never marry.'

'Because –' Maisie left the sentence unfinished, looking at her friend. The latter gave a short nod of assent.

Footsteps were heard on the stairs. The butler threw open the door and announced:

'Mr Segrave.'

John came in without any particular enthusiasm. He couldn't imagine why the old boy had asked him. If he could have got out of it he would have done so. The house depressed him, with its solid magnificence and the soft pile of its carpet.

A girl came forward and shook hands with him. He remembered vaguely having seen her one day in her father's office.

'How do you do, Mr Segrave? Mr Segrave – Miss Kerr.'

Then he woke. Who was she? Where did she come from? From the flame-coloured draperies that floated round her, to the tiny Mercury wings on her small

21

Greek head, she was a being transitory and fugitive, standing out against the dull background with an effect of unreality.

Rudolf Wetterman came in, his broad expanse of gleaming shirt-front creaking as he walked. They went down informally to dinner.

Allegra Kerr talked to her host. John Segrave had to devote himself to Maisie. But his whole mind was on the girl on the other side of him. She was marvellously effective. Her effectiveness was, he thought, more studied than natural. But behind all that, there lay something else. Flickering fire, fitful, capricious, like the will-o'-the-wisps that of old lured men into the marshes.

At last he got a chance to speak to her. Maisie was giving her father a message from some friend she had met that day. Now that the moment had come, he was tongue-tied. His glance pleaded with her dumbly.

'Dinner-table topics,' she said lightly. 'Shall we start with the theatres, or with one of those innumerable openings beginning, "Do you like –?"'

John laughed.

'And if we find we both like dogs and dislike sandy cats, it will form what is called a "bond" between us?'

'Assuredly,' said Allegra gravely.

'It is, I think, a pity to begin with a catechism.'

'Yet it puts conversation within the reach of all.'

'True, but with disastrous results.'

'It is useful to know the rules – if only to break them.'

John smiled at her.

'I take it, then, that you and I will indulge our personal vagaries. Even though we display thereby the genius that is akin to madness.'

With a sharp unguarded movement, the girl's hand swept a wineglass off the table. There was the tinkle of broken glass. Maisie and her father stopped speaking.

'I'm so sorry, Mr Wetterman. I'm throwing glasses on the floor.'

'My dear Allegra, it doesn't matter at all, not at all.'

Beneath his breath John Segrave said quickly:

'Broken glass. That's bad luck. I wish – it hadn't happened.'

'Don't worry. How does it go? "Ill luck thou canst not bring where ill luck has its home."'

She turned once more to Wetterman. John, resuming conversation with Maisie, tried to place the quotation. He got it at last. They were the words used by Sieglinde in the Walküre when Sigmund offers to leave the house.

He thought: 'Did she mean –?'

But Maisie was asking his opinion of the latest

Revue. Soon he had admitted that he was fond of music.

'After dinner,' said Maisie, 'we'll make Allegra play for us.'

They all went up to the drawing-room together. Secretly, Wetterman considered it a barbarous custom. He liked the ponderous gravity of the wine passing round, the handed cigars. But perhaps it was as well tonight. He didn't know what on earth he could find to say to young Segrave. Maisie was too bad with her whims. It wasn't as though the fellow were good looking – really good looking – and certainly he wasn't amusing. He was glad when Maisie asked Allegra Kerr to play. They'd get through the evening sooner. The young idiot didn't even play Bridge.

Allegra played well, though without the sure touch of a professional. She played modern music, Debussy and Strauss, a little Scriabin. Then she dropped into the first movement of Beethoven's *Pathétique*, that expression of a grief that is infinite, a sorrow that is endless and vast as the ages, but in which from end to end breathes the spirit that will not accept defeat. In the solemnity of undying woe, it moves with the rhythm of the conqueror to its final doom.

Towards the end she faltered, her fingers struck a discord, and she broke off abruptly. She looked across at Maisie and laughed mockingly.

'You see,' she said. 'They won't let me.'

Then, without waiting for a reply to her somewhat enigmatical remark, she plunged into a strange haunting melody, a thing of weird harmonies and curious measured rhythm, quite unlike anything Segrave had ever heard before. It was delicate as the flight of a bird, poised, hovering – suddenly, without the least warning, it turned into a mere discordant jangle of notes, and Allegra rose laughing from the piano.

In spite of her laugh, she looked disturbed and almost frightened. She sat down by Maisie, and John heard the latter say in a low tone to her:

'You shouldn't do it. You really shouldn't do it.'

'What was the last thing?' John asked eagerly.

'Something of my own.'

She spoke sharply and curtly. Wetterman changed the subject.

That night John Segrave dreamt again of the House.

III

John was unhappy. His life was irksome to him as never before. Up to now he had accepted it patiently – a disagreeable necessity, but one which left his inner freedom essentially untouched. Now all that was changed. The outer world and the inner intermingled.

He did not disguise to himself the reason for the change. He had fallen in love at first sight with Allegra Kerr. What was he going to do about it?

He had been too bewildered that first night to make any plans. He had not even tried to see her again. A little later, when Maisie Wetterman asked him down to her father's place in the country for a weekend, he went eagerly, but he was disappointed, for Allegra was not there.

He mentioned her once, tentatively, to Maisie, and she told him that Allegra was up in Scotland paying a visit. He left it at that. He would have liked to go on talking about her, but the words seemed to stick in his throat.

Maisie was puzzled by him that weekend. He didn't appear to see – well, to see what was so plainly to be seen. She was a direct young woman in her methods, but directness was lost upon John. He thought her kind, but a little overpowering.

Yet the Fates were stronger than Maisie. They willed that John should see Allegra again.

They met in the park one Sunday afternoon. He had seen her from far off, and his heart thumped against the side of his ribs. Supposing she should have forgotten him –

But she had not forgotten. She stopped and spoke.

In a few minutes they were walking side by side, striking out across the grass. He was ridiculously happy.

He said suddenly and unexpectedly:

'Do you believe in dreams?'

'I believe in nightmares.'

The harshness of her voice startled him.

'Nightmares,' he said stupidly. 'I didn't mean nightmares.'

Allegra looked at him.

'No,' she said. 'There have been no nightmares in your life. I can see that.'

Her voice was gentle – different.

He told her then of his dream of the white house, stammering a little. He had had it now six – no, seven times. Always the same. It was beautiful – so beautiful!

He went on.

'You see – it's to do with *you* – in some way. I had it first the night before I met you.'

'To do with me?' She laughed – a short bitter laugh. 'Oh, no, that's impossible. The house was beautiful.'

'So are you,' said John Segrave.

Allegra flushed a little with annoyance.

'I'm sorry – I was stupid. I seemed to ask for a compliment, didn't I? But I didn't really mean that at all. The outside of me is all right, I know.'

'I haven't seen the inside of the house yet,' said John

Segrave. 'When I do I know it will be quite as beautiful as the outside.'

He spoke slowly and gravely, giving the words a meaning that she chose to ignore.

'There is something more I want to tell you – if you will listen.'

'I will listen,' said Allegra.

'I am chucking up this job of mine. I ought to have done it long ago – I see that now. I have been content to drift along knowing I was an utter failure, without caring much, just living from day to day. A man shouldn't do that. It's a man's business to find something he can do and make a success of it. I'm chucking this, and taking on something else – quite a different sort of thing. It's a kind of expedition in West Africa – I can't tell you the details. They're not supposed to be known; but if it comes off – well, I shall be a rich man.'

'So you, too, count success in terms of money?'

'Money,' said John Segrave, 'means just one thing to me – you! When I come back –' he paused.

She bent her head. Her face had grown very pale.

'I won't pretend to misunderstand. That's why I must tell you now, once and for all: *I shall never marry.*'

He stayed a little while considering, then he said very gently:

'Can't you tell me why?'

'I could, but more than anything in the world I do not want to tell you.'

Again he was silent, then he looked up suddenly and a singularly attractive smile illumined his faun's face.

'I see,' he said. 'So you won't let me come inside the House – not even to peep in for a second? The blinds are to stay down.'

Allegra leaned forward and laid her hand on his.

'I will tell you this much. You dream of your House. But I – don't dream. My dreams are nightmares!'

And on that she left him, abruptly, disconcertingly.

That night, once more, he dreamed. Of late, he had realized that the House was most certainly tenanted. He had seen a hand draw aside the blinds, had caught glimpses of moving figures within.

Tonight the House seemed fairer than it had ever done before. Its white walls shone in the sunlight. The peace and the beauty of it were complete.

Then, suddenly, he became aware of a fuller ripple of the waves of joy. Someone was coming to the window. He knew it. A hand, the same hand that he had seen before, laid hold of the blind, drawing it back. In a minute he would see . . .

He was awake – still quivering with the horror, the unutterable loathing of the *Thing* that had looked out at him from the window of the House.

It was a Thing utterly and wholly horrible, a Thing

so vile and loathsome that the mere remembrance of it made him feel sick. And he knew that the most unutterably and horribly vile thing about it was its presence in that House – the House of Beauty.

For where that Thing abode was horror – horror that rose up and slew the peace and the serenity which were the birthright of the House. The beauty, the wonderful immortal beauty of the House was destroyed for ever, for within its holy consecrated walls there dwelt the Shadow of an Unclean Thing!

If ever again he should dream of the House, Segrave knew he would awake at once with a start of terror, lest from its white beauty that Thing might suddenly look out at him.

The following evening, when he left the office, he went straight to the Wettermans' house. He must see Allegra Kerr. Maisie would tell him where she was to be found.

He never noticed the eager light that flashed into Maisie's eyes as he was shown in, and she jumped up to greet him. He stammered out his request at once, with her hand still in his.

'Miss Kerr. I met her yesterday, but I don't know where she's staying.'

He did not feel Maisie's hand grow limp in his as she withdrew it. The sudden coldness of her voice told him nothing.

'Allegra is here – staying with us. But I'm afraid you can't see her.'

'But –'

'You see, her mother died this morning. We've just had the news.'

'Oh!' He was taken aback.

'It is all very sad,' said Maisie. She hesitated just a minute, then went on. 'You see, she died in – well, practically an asylum. There's insanity in the family. The grandfather shot himself, and one of Allegra's aunts is a hopeless imbecile, and another drowned herself.'

John Segrave made an inarticulate sound.

'I thought I ought to tell you,' said Maisie virtuously. 'We're such friends, aren't we? And of course Allegra is very attractive. Lots of people have asked her to marry them, but naturally she won't marry at all – she couldn't, could she?'

'She's all right,' said Segrave. 'There's nothing wrong with *her*.'

His voice sounded hoarse and unnatural in his own ears.

'One never knows, her mother was quite all right when she was young. And she wasn't just – peculiar, you know. She was quite raving mad. It's a dreadful thing – insanity.'

'Yes,' he said, 'it's a most awful Thing.'

He knew now what it was that had looked at him from the window of the House.

Maisie was still talking on. He interrupted her brusquely.

'I really came to say goodbye – and to thank you for all your kindness.'

'You're not – going away?'

There was alarm in her voice.

He smiled sideways at her – a crooked smile, pathetic and attractive.

'Yes,' he said. 'To Africa.'

'Africa!'

Maisie echoed the word blankly. Before she could pull herself together he had shaken her by the hand and gone. She was left standing there, her hands clenched by her sides, an angry spot of colour in each cheek.

Below, on the doorstep, John Segrave came face to face with Allegra coming in from the street. She was in black, her face white and lifeless. She took one glance at him then drew him into a small morning room.

'Maisie told you,' she said. 'You *know*?'

He nodded.

'But what does it matter? *You're* all right. It – it leaves some people out.'

She looked at him sombrely, mournfully.

'You *are* all right,' he repeated.

'I don't know,' she almost whispered it. 'I don't

know. I told you – about my dreams. And when I play – when I'm at the piano – *those others* come and take hold of my hands.'

He was staring at her – paralysed. For one instant, as she spoke, something looked out from her eyes. It was gone in a flash – but he knew it. It was the Thing that had looked out from the House.

She caught his momentary recoil.

'You see,' she whispered. 'You see – but I wish Maisie hadn't told you. It takes everything from you.'

'Everything?'

'Yes. There won't even be the dreams left. For now – you'll never dare to dream of the House again.'

IV

The West African sun poured down, and the heat was intense.

John Segrave continued to moan.

'I can't find it. I can't find it.'

The little English doctor with the red head and the tremendous jaw, scowled down upon his patient in that bullying manner which he had made his own.

'He's always saying that. What does he mean?'

'He speaks, I think, of a house, monsieur.' The soft-voiced Sister of Charity from the Roman Catholic

Agatha Christie

Mission spoke with her gentle detachment, as she too looked down on the stricken man.

'A house, eh? Well, he's got to get it out of his head, or we shan't pull him through. It's on his mind. Segrave! Segrave!'

The wandering attention was fixed. The eyes rested with recognition on the doctor's face.

'Look here, you're going to pull through. I'm going to pull you through. But you've got to stop worrying about this house. It can't run away, you know. So don't bother about looking for it now.'

'All right.' He seemed obedient. 'I suppose it can't very well run away if it's never been there at all.'

'Of course not!' The doctor laughed his cheery laugh. 'Now you'll be all right in no time.' And with a boisterous bluntness of manner he took his departure.

Segrave lay thinking. The fever had abated for the moment, and he could think clearly and lucidly. He *must* find that House.

For ten years he had dreaded finding it – the thought that he might come upon it unawares had been his greatest terror. And then, he remembered, when his fears were quite lulled to rest, one day *it* had found *him*. He recalled clearly his first haunting terror, and then his sudden, his exquisite, relief. For, after all, the House was empty!

Quite empty and exquisitely peaceful. It was as he

remembered it ten years before. He had not forgotten. There was a huge black furniture van moving slowly away from the House. The last tenant, of course, moving out with his goods. He went up to the men in charge of the van and spoke to them. There was something rather sinister about that van, it was so very black. The horses were black, too, with freely flowing manes and tails, and the men all wore black clothes and gloves. It all reminded him of something else, something that he couldn't remember.

Yes, he had been quite right. The last tenant was moving out, as his lease was up. The House was to stand empty for the present, until the owner came back from abroad.

And waking, he had been full of the peaceful beauty of the empty House.

A month after that, he had received a letter from Maisie (she wrote to him perseveringly, once a month). In it she told him that Allegra Kerr had died in the same home as her mother, and wasn't it dreadfully sad? Though of course a merciful release.

It had really been very odd indeed. Coming after his dream like that. He didn't quite understand it all. But it was odd.

And the worst of it was that he'd never been able to find the House since. Somehow, he'd forgotten the way.

The fever began to take hold of him once more. He tossed restlessly. Of course, he'd forgotten, the House was on high ground! He must climb to get there. But it was hot work climbing cliffs – dreadfully hot. Up, up, up – oh! he had slipped! He must start again from the bottom. Up, up, up – days passed, weeks – he wasn't sure that years didn't go by! And he was still climbing.

Once he heard the doctor's voice. But he couldn't stop climbing to listen. Besides the doctor would tell him to leave off looking for the House. *He* thought it was an ordinary house. He didn't know.

He remembered suddenly that he must be calm, very calm. You couldn't find the House unless you were very calm. It was no use looking for the House in a hurry, or being excited.

If he could only keep calm! But it was so hot! Hot? It was *cold* – yes, cold. These weren't cliffs, they were icebergs – jagged cold, icebergs.

He was so tired. He wouldn't go on looking – it was no good. Ah! here was a lane – that was better than icebergs, anyway. How pleasant and shady it was in the cool, green lane. And those trees – they were splendid! They were rather like – what? He couldn't remember, but it didn't matter.

Ah! here were flowers. All golden and blue! How lovely it all was – and how strangely familiar. Of course, he had been here before. There, through the trees, was the gleam of the House, standing on the high ground. How beautiful it was. The green lane and the trees and the flowers were as nothing to the paramount, the all-satisfying, beauty of the House.

He hastened his steps. To think that he had never yet been inside! How unbelievably stupid of him – when he had the key in his pocket all the time!

And of course the beauty of the exterior was as nothing to the beauty that lay within – especially now that the owner had come back from abroad. He mounted the steps to the great door.

Cruel strong hands were dragging him back! They fought him, dragging him to and fro, backwards and forwards.

The doctor was shaking him, roaring in his ear. 'Hold on, man, you can. Don't let go. Don't let go.' His eyes were alight with the fierceness of one who sees an enemy. Segrave wondered who the Enemy was. The black-robed nun was praying. That, too, was strange.

And all *he* wanted was to be left alone. To go back to the House. For every minute the House was growing fainter.

That, of course, was because the doctor was so strong. He wasn't strong enough to fight the doctor. If he only could.

But stop! There was another way – the way dreams

went in the moment of waking. No strength could stop *them* – they just flitted past. The doctor's hands wouldn't be able to hold him if he slipped – just slipped!

Yes, that was the way! The white walls were visible once more, the doctor's voice was fainter, his hands were barely felt. He knew now how dreams laugh when they give you the slip!

He was at the door of the House. The exquisite stillness was unbroken. He put the key in the lock and turned it.

Just a moment he waited, to realize to the full the perfect, the ineffable, the all-satisfying completeness of joy.

Then – he passed over the Threshold.

Afterword

'The House of Dreams' was first published in the *Sovereign Magazine* in January 1926. The story is a revised version of 'The House of Beauty', which Christie wrote some time before the First World War and identified in her autobiography as being 'the first thing I ever wrote that showed any sign of promise'. Whereas the original story was obscure and excessively morbid in tone, 'The House of Dreams' comes close to the threatening ghost stories of the Edwardian age, and especially those of E. F. Benson. It is a great deal clearer and less introspective than the original which Christie heavily revised for publication: to develop the characters of the two women she toned down the otherworldliness of Allegra and built up Maisie's rôle. A similar theme is explored in 'The Call of Wings', another early story, collected in *The Hound of Death* (1933).

Agatha Christie

In 1938, Christie reflected on 'The House of Beauty', recalling that, while she had found 'the imagining of it pleasant and the writing of it down extremely tedious', the seed had been sown – 'The pastime grew on me. When I had a blank day – nothing much to do – I would think out a story. They always had sad endings and sometimes very lofty moral sentiments.' An important spur in these early years was a neighbour on Dartmoor, Eden Phillpotts, a celebrated novelist and a close friend of the family, who advised Christie – Agatha Miller as she was then – on her stories and recommended writers whose style and vocabulary were to provide added inspiration. In later years, when her own fame had long since eclipsed his, Christie described how Phillpotts had provided the tact and sympathy so necessary to sustain the confidence of a young writer – 'I marvel at the understanding with which he doled out only encouragement and refrained from criticism.' On Phillpotts' death in 1960, she wrote, 'For his kindness to me as a young girl just beginning to write, I can never be sufficiently grateful.'

The Actress

I

The shabby man in the fourth row of the pit leant forward and stared incredulously at the stage. His shifty eyes narrowed furtively.

'Nancy Taylor!' he muttered. 'By the Lord, little Nancy Taylor!'

His glance dropped to the programme in his hand. One name was printed in slightly larger type than the rest.

'Olga Stormer! So that's what she calls herself. Fancy yourself a star, don't you, my lady? And you must be making a pretty little pot of money, too. Quite forgotten your name was ever Nancy Taylor, I daresay. I wonder now – I wonder now what you'd say if Jake Levitt should remind you of the fact?'

The curtain fell on the close of the first act. Hearty applause filled the auditorium. Olga Stormer, the great emotional actress, whose name in a few short years had become a household word, was adding yet another triumph to her list of successes as 'Cora', in *The Avenging Angel*.

Jake Levitt did not join in the clapping, but a slow, appreciative grin gradually distended his mouth. God! What luck! Just when he was on his beam-ends, too. She'd try to bluff it out, he supposed, but she couldn't put it over on *him*. Properly worked, the thing was a gold-mine!

II

On the following morning the first workings of Jake Levitt's gold-mine became apparent. In her drawing-room, with its red lacquer and black hangings, Olga Stormer read and re-read a letter thoughtfully. Her pale face, with its exquisitely mobile features, was a little more set than usual, and every now and then the grey-green eyes under the level brows steadily envisaged the middle distance, as though she contemplated the threat behind rather than the actual words of the letter.

In that wonderful voice of hers which could throb with emotion or be as clear-cut as the click of a typewriter, Olga called: 'Miss Jones!'

A neat young woman with spectacles, a shorthand

pad and a pencil clasped in her hand, hastened from an adjoining room.

'Ring up Mr Danahan, please, and ask him to come round, immediately.'

Syd Danahan, Olga Stormer's manager, entered the room with the usual apprehension of the man whose life it is to deal with and overcome the vagaries of the artistic feminine. To coax, to soothe, to bully, one at a time or all together, such was his daily routine. To his relief, Olga appeared calm and composed, and merely flicked a note across the table to him.

'Read that.'

The letter was scrawled in an illiterate hand, on cheap paper.

> *'Dear Madam,*
>
> *I much appreciated your performance in* The Avenging Angel *last night. I fancy we have a mutual friend in Miss Nancy Taylor, late of Chicago. An article regarding her is to be published shortly. If you would care to discuss same, I could call upon you at any time convenient to yourself.*
>
> *Yours respectfully,*
> *Jake Levitt'*

Danahan looked slightly bewildered.

'I don't quite get it. Who is this Nancy Taylor?'

'A girl who would be better dead, Danny.' There was

bitterness in her voice and a weariness that revealed her thirty-four years. 'A girl who was dead until this carrion crow brought her to life again.'

'Oh! Then . . .'

'Me, Danny. Just me.'

'This means blackmail, of course?'

She nodded. 'Of course, and by a man who knows the art thoroughly.'

Danahan frowned, considering the matter. Olga, her cheek pillowed on a long, slender hand, watched him with unfathomable eyes.

'What about bluff? Deny everything. He can't be sure that he hasn't been misled by a chance resemblance.'

Olga shook her head.

'Levitt makes his living by blackmailing women. He's sure enough.'

'The police?' hinted Danahan doubtfully.

Her faint, derisive smile was answer enough. Beneath her self-control, though he did not guess it, was the impatience of the keen brain watching a slower brain laboriously cover the ground it had already traversed in a flash.

'You don't – er – think it might be wise for you to – er – say something yourself to Sir Richard? That would partly spike his guns.'

The actress's engagement to Sir Richard Everard, MP, had been announced a few weeks previously.

'I told Richard everything when he asked me to marry him.'

'My word, that was clever of you!' said Danahan admiringly.

Olga smiled a little.

'It wasn't cleverness, Danny dear. You wouldn't understand. All the same, if this man Levitt does what he threatens, my number is up, and incidentally Richard's Parliamentary career goes smash, too. No, as far as I can see, there are only two things to do.'

'Well?'

'To pay – and that of course is endless! Or to disappear, start again.'

The weariness was again very apparent in her voice.

'It isn't even as though I'd done anything I regretted. I was a half-starved little gutter waif, Danny, striving to keep straight. I shot a man, a beast of a man who deserved to be shot. The circumstances under which I killed him were such that no jury on earth would have convicted me. I know that now, but at the time I was only a frightened kid – and – I ran.'

Danahan nodded.

'I suppose,' he said doubtfully, 'there's nothing against this man Levitt we could get hold of?'

Olga shook her head.

'Very unlikely. He's too much of a coward to go in for evil-doing.' The sound of her own words seemed to strike her. 'A coward! I wonder if we couldn't work on that in some way.'

'If Sir Richard were to see him and frighten him,' suggested Danahan.

'Richard is too fine an instrument. You can't handle that sort of man with gloves on.'

'Well, let me see him.'

'Forgive me, Danny, but I don't think you're subtle enough. Something between gloves and bare fists is needed. Let us say mittens! That means a woman! Yes, I rather fancy a woman might do the trick. A woman with a certain amount of *finesse*, but who knows the baser side of life from bitter experience. Olga Stormer, for instance! Don't talk to me, I've got a plan coming.'

She leant forward, burying her face in her hands. She lifted it suddenly.

'What's the name of that girl who wants to understudy me? Margaret Ryan, isn't it? The girl with the hair like mine?'

'Her hair's all right,' admitted Danahan grudgingly, his eyes resting on the bronze-gold coil surrounding Olga's head. 'It's just like yours, as you say. But she's no good any other way. I was going to sack her next week.'

'If all goes well, you'll probably have to let her understudy "Cora".' She smothered his protests with a wave of her hand. 'Danny, answer me one question honestly. Do you think I can act? Really *act*, I mean. Or am I just an attractive woman who trails round in pretty dresses?'

'Act? My God! Olga, there's been nobody like you since Duse!'

'Then if Levitt is really a coward, as I suspect, the thing will come off. No, I'm not going to tell you about it. I want you to get hold of the Ryan girl. Tell her I'm interested in her and want her to dine here tomorrow night. She'll come fast enough.'

'I should say she would!'

'The other thing I want is some good strong knock-out drops, something that will put anyone out of action for an hour or two, but leave them none the worse the next day.'

Danahan grinned.

'I can't guarantee our friend won't have a headache, but there will be no permanent damage done.'

'Good! Run away now, Danny, and leave the rest to me.' She raised her voice: 'Miss Jones!'

The spectacled young woman appeared with her usual alacrity.

'Take down this, please.'

Walking slowly up and down, Olga dictated the day's correspondence. But one answer she wrote with her own hand.

47

Jake Levitt, in his dingy room, grinned as he tore open the expected envelope.

'Dear Sir,
   I cannot recall the lady of whom you speak, but I meet so many people that my memory is necessarily uncertain. I am always pleased to help any fellow actress, and shall be at home if you will call this evening at nine o'clock.
   Yours faithfully,
   Olga Stormer'

Levitt nodded appreciatively. Clever note! She admitted nothing. Nevertheless she was willing to treat. The gold-mine was developing.

III

At nine o'clock precisely Levitt stood outside the door of the actress's flat and pressed the bell. No one answered the summons, and he was about to press it again when he realized that the door was not latched. He pushed the door open and entered the hall. To his right was an open door leading into a brilliantly lighted room, a room decorated in scarlet and black. Levitt walked in. On the table under the lamp lay a sheet of paper on which were written the words:

'Please wait until I return. – O. Stormer.'

Levitt sat down and waited. In spite of himself a feeling of uneasiness was stealing over him. The flat was so very quiet. There was something eerie about the silence.

Nothing wrong, of course, how could there be? But the room was so deadly quiet; and yet, quiet as it was, he had the preposterous, uncomfortable notion that he wasn't alone in it. Absurd! He wiped the perspiration from his brow. And still the impression grew stronger. He wasn't alone! With a muttered oath he sprang up and began to pace up and down. In a minute the woman would return and then –

He stopped dead with a muffled cry. From beneath the black velvet hangings that draped the window a hand protruded! He stooped and touched it. Cold – horribly cold – a dead hand.

With a cry he flung back the curtains. A woman was lying there, one arm flung wide, the other doubled under her as she lay face downwards, her golden-bronze hair lying in dishevelled masses on her neck.

Olga Stormer! Tremblingly his fingers sought the icy coldness of that wrist and felt for the pulse. As he thought, there was none. She was dead. She had escaped him, then, by taking the simplest way out.

Suddenly his eyes were arrested by two ends of red

cord finishing in fantastic tassels, and half hidden by the masses of her hair. He touched them gingerly; the head sagged as he did so, and he caught a glimpse of a horrible purple face. He sprang back with a cry, his head whirling. There was something here he did not understand. His brief glimpse of the face, disfigured as it was, had shown him one thing. This was murder, not suicide. The woman had been strangled and – she was not Olga Stormer!

Ah! What was that? A sound behind him. He wheeled round and looked straight into the terrified eyes of a maid-servant crouching against the wall. Her face was as white as the cap and apron she wore, but he did not understand the fascinated horror in her eyes until her half-breathed words enlightened him to the peril in which he stood.

'Oh, my Gord! You've killed 'er!'

Even then he did not quite realize. He replied:

'No, no, she was dead when I found her.'

'I saw yer do it! You pulled the cord and strangled her. I 'eard the gurgling cry she give.'

The sweat broke out upon his brow in earnest. His mind went rapidly over his actions of the previous few minutes. She must have come in just as he had the two ends of cord in his hands; she had seen the sagging head and had taken his own cry as coming from the victim. He stared at her helplessly. There was no doubting what he saw in her face – terror and stupidity. She would tell the police she had seen the crime committed, and no cross-examination would shake her, he was sure of that. She would swear away his life with the unshakable conviction that she was speaking the truth.

What a horrible, unforeseen chain of circumstances! Stop, was it unforeseen? Was there some devilry here? On an impulse he said, eyeing her narrowly:

'That's not your mistress, you know.'

Her answer, given mechanically, threw a light upon the situation.

'No, it's 'er actress friend – if you can call 'em friends, seeing that they fought like cat and dog. They were at it tonight, 'ammer and tongs.'

A trap! He saw it now.

'Where's your mistress?'

'Went out ten minutes ago.'

A trap! And he had walked into it like a lamb. A clever devil, this Olga Stormer; she had rid herself of a rival, and he was to suffer for the deed. Murder! My God, they hanged a man for murder! And he was innocent – innocent!

A stealthy rustle recalled him. The little maid was sidling towards the door. Her wits were beginning to work again. Her eyes wavered to the telephone, then back to the door. At all costs he must silence her. It was the only way. As well hang for a real crime as a fictitious one. She had no weapon, neither had he. But he had his hands! Then his heart gave a leap. On the table beside her, almost under her hand, lay a small, jewelled revolver. If he could reach it first –

Instinct or his eyes warned her. She caught it up as he sprang and held it pointed at his breast. Awkwardly as she held it, her finger was on the trigger, and she could hardly miss him at that distance. He stopped dead. A revolver belonging to a woman like Olga Stormer would be pretty sure to be loaded.

But there was one thing, she was no longer directly between him and the door. So long as he did not attack her, she might not have the nerve to shoot. Anyway, he must risk it. Zig-zagging, he ran for the door, through the hall and out through the outer door, banging it behind him. He heard her voice, faint and shaky, calling, 'Police, Murder!' She'd have to call louder than that before anyone was likely to hear her. He'd got a start, anyway. Down the stairs he went, running down the open street, then slacking to a walk as a stray pedestrian turned the corner. He had his plan cut and dried. To Gravesend as quickly as possible. A boat was sailing from there that night for the remoter parts of the world. He knew the captain, a man who, for a consideration, would ask no question. Once on board and out to sea he would be safe.

IV

At eleven o'clock Danahan's telephone rang. Olga's voice spoke.

'Prepare a contract for Miss Ryan, will you? She's to understudy "Cora". It's absolutely no use arguing. I owe her something after all the things I did to her tonight! What? Yes, I think I'm out of my troubles. By the way, if she tells you tomorrow that I'm an ardent spiritualist and put her into a trance tonight, don't show open incredulity. How? Knock-out drops in the coffee, followed by scientific passes! After that I painted her face with purple grease paint and put a tourniquet on her left arm! Mystified? Well, you must stay mystified until tomorrow. I haven't time to explain now. I must get out of the cap and apron before my faithful Maud returns from the pictures. There was a "beautiful drama" on tonight, she told me. But she missed the best drama of all. I played my best part tonight, Danny. The mittens won! Jake Levitt is a coward all right, and oh, Danny, Danny – I'm an actress!'

Afterword

'The Actress' was first published in the *Novel Magazine* in May 1923 as 'A Trap for the Unwary', the title under which it was re-published in the booklet issued in 1990 to mark the centenary of Christie's birth.

This story illustrates Christie's great skill at taking a particular plot device and presenting it again, perhaps in the same form but from a different perspective or with subtle but significant variations to conceal it from the reader. The simple piece of legerdemain in 'The Actress' appears in several other stories, most obviously in the intriguing Miss Marple story 'The Affair at the Bungalow', collected in *The Thirteen Problems* (1932), and in the Poirot novel *Evil Under the Sun* (1941).

This story reminds us that Christie is also one of Britain's most successful playwrights, even though her first play – which she described as 'an enormously gloomy play which, if my memory serves me correct, was about incest' – was never performed. Her own favourite was *Witness for the Prosecution* (1953) but the most famous is undoubtedly *The Mousetrap* (1952), which is still running in London after nearly 50 years. While the plot of *The Mousetrap* centres on a murderer's ability to deceive his potential victims, it depends as a piece of theatre on Christie's awareness of how people in an audience respond to what they see and hear and her supreme ability to manipulate what they then understand to be happening. After *The Mousetrap* opened in London, the reviewer in *The Times* commented that 'the piece admirably fulfils the special requirements of the theatre' and, as anyone who has been associated with the play or has studied it carefully knows well, there *is* a secret to its success, or rather to the success of why so few are able to foresee its astounding denouement.

The Edge

I

Clare Halliwell walked down the short path that led from her cottage door to the gate. On her arm was a basket, and in the basket was a bottle of soup, some homemade jelly and a few grapes. There were not many poor people in the small village of Daymer's End, but such as there were were assiduously looked after, and Clare was one of the most efficient of the parish workers.

Clare Halliwell was thirty-two. She had an upright carriage, a healthy colour and nice brown eyes. She was not beautiful, but she looked fresh and pleasant and very English. Everybody liked her, and said she was a good sort. Since her mother's death, two years ago, she had lived alone in the cottage with her dog, Rover. She kept poultry and was fond of animals and of a healthy outdoor life.

As she unlatched the gate, a two-seater car swept

past, and the driver, a girl in a red hat, waved a greeting. Clare responded, but for a moment her lips tightened. She felt that pang at her heart which always came when she saw Vivien Lee. Gerald's wife!

Medenham Grange, which lay just a mile outside the village, had belonged to the Lees for many generations. Sir Gerald Lee, the present owner of the Grange, was a man old for his years and considered by many stiff in manner. His pomposity really covered a good deal of shyness. He and Clare had played together as children. Later they had been friends, and a closer and dearer tie had been confidently expected by many – including, it may be said, Clare herself. There was no hurry, of course – but some day . . . She left it so in her own mind. Some day.

And then, just a year ago, the village had been startled by the news of Sir Gerald's marriage to a Miss Harper – a girl nobody had ever heard of!

The new Lady Lee had not been popular in the village. She took not the faintest interest in parochial matters, was bored by hunting, and loathed the country and outdoor sports. Many of the wiseacres shook their heads and wondered how it would end. It was easy to see where Sir Gerald's infatuation had come in. Vivien was a beauty. From head to foot she was a complete contrast to Clare Halliwell, small, elfin, dainty, with golden-red hair that curled enchantingly over her pretty ears, and big violet eyes that could shoot a sideways glance of provocation to the manner born.

Gerald Lee, in his simple man's way, had been anxious that his wife and Clare should be great friends. Clare was often asked to dine at the Grange, and Vivien made a pretty pretence of affectionate intimacy whenever they met. Hence that gay salutation of hers this morning.

Clare walked on and did her errand. The Vicar was also visiting the old woman in question and he and Clare walked a few yards together afterwards before their ways parted. They stood still for a minute discussing parish affairs.

'Jones has broken out again, I'm afraid,' said the Vicar. 'And I had such hopes after he had volunteered, of his own accord, to take the pledge.'

'Disgusting,' said Clare crisply.

'It seems so to us,' said Mr Wilmot, 'but we must remember that it is very hard to put ourselves in his place and realize his temptation. The desire for drink is unaccountable to us, but we all have our own temptations, and thus we can understand.'

'I suppose we have,' said Clare uncertainly.

The Vicar glanced at her.

'Some of us have the good fortune to be very little tempted,' he said gently. 'But even to those people their hour comes. Watch and pray, remember, that ye enter not into temptation.'

Then bidding her goodbye, he walked briskly away. Clare went on thoughtfully, and presently she almost bumped into Sir Gerald Lee.

'Hullo, Clare. I was hoping to run across you. You look jolly fit. What a colour you've got.'

The colour had not been there a minute before. Lee went on:

'As I say, I was hoping to run across you. Vivien's got to go off to Bournemouth for the weekend. Her mother's not well. Can you dine with us Tuesday instead of tonight?'

'Oh, yes! Tuesday will suit me just as well.'

'That's all right, then. Splendid. I must hurry along.'

Clare went home to find her one faithful domestic standing on the doorstep looking out for her.

'There you are, Miss. Such a to-do. They've brought Rover home. He went off on his own this morning, and a car ran clean over him.'

Clare hurried to the dog's side. She adored animals, and Rover was her especial darling. She felt his legs one by one, and then ran her hands over his body. He groaned once or twice and licked her hand.

'If there's any serious injury, it's internal,' she said at last. 'No bones seem to be broken.'

'Shall we get the vet to see him, Miss?'

Clare shook her head. She had little faith in the local vet.

'We'll wait until tomorrow. He doesn't seem to be in great pain, and his gums are a good colour, so there can't be much internal bleeding. Tomorrow, if I don't like the look of him, I'll take him over to Skippington in the car and let Reeves have a look at him. He's far and away the best man.'

II

On the following day, Rover seemed weaker, and Clare duly carried out her project. The small town of Skippington was about forty miles away, a long run, but Reeves, the vet there, was celebrated for many miles round.

He diagnosed certain internal injuries, but held out good hopes of recovery, and Clare went away quite content to leave Rover in his charge.

There was only one hotel of any pretensions in Skippington, the *County Arms*. It was mainly frequented by commercial travellers, for there was no good hunting country near Skippington, and it was off the track of the main roads for motorists.

Lunch was not served till one o'clock, and as it wanted a few minutes of that hour, Clare amused

herself by glancing over the entries in the open visitors'
book.

Suddenly she gave a stifled exclamation. Surely she
knew that handwriting, with its loops and whirls and
flourishes? She had always considered it unmistakable.
Even now she could have sworn – but of course it was
clearly impossible. Vivien Lee was at Bournemouth.
The entry itself showed it to be impossible:

Mr and Mrs Cyril Brown. London.

But in spite of herself her eyes strayed back again
and again to that curly writing, and on an impulse she
could not quite define she asked abruptly of the woman
in the office:

'Mrs Cyril Brown? I wonder if that is the same one
I know?'

'A small lady? Reddish hair? Very pretty. She came
in a red two-seater car, madam. A Peugeot, I believe.'

Then it was! A coincidence would be too remarkable.
As if in a dream, she heard the woman go on:

'They were here just over a month ago for a weekend,
and liked it so much that they have come again. Newly
married, I should fancy.'

Clare heard herself saying: 'Thank you. I don't think
that could be my friend.'

Her voice sounded different, as though it belonged

to someone else. Presently she was sitting in the dining-room, quietly eating cold roast beef, her mind a maze of conflicting thought and emotions.

She had no doubts whatever. She had summed Vivien up pretty correctly on their first meeting. Vivien was that kind. She wondered vaguely who the man was. Someone Vivien had known before her marriage? Very likely – it didn't matter – nothing mattered, but Gerald.

What was she – Clare – to do about Gerald? He ought to know – surely he ought to know. It was clearly her duty to tell him. She had discovered Vivien's secret by accident, but she must lose no time in acquainting Gerald with the facts. She was Gerald's friend, not Vivien's.

But somehow or other she felt uncomfortable. Her conscience was not satisfied. On the face of it, her reasoning was good, but duty and inclination jumped suspiciously together. She admitted to herself that she disliked Vivien. Besides, if Gerald Lee were to divorce his wife – and Clare had no doubts at all that that was exactly what he would do, he was a man with an almost fanatical view of his own honour – then – well, the way would lie open for Gerald to come to her. Put like that, she shrank back fastidiously. Her own proposed action seemed naked and ugly.

The personal element entered in too much. She could not be sure of her own motives. Clare was essentially a high-minded, conscientious woman. She strove now very earnestly to see where her duty lay. She wished, as she had always wished, to do right. What was right in this case? What was wrong?

By a pure accident she had come into possession of facts that affected vitally the man she loved and the woman whom she disliked and – yes, one might as well be frank – of whom she was bitterly jealous. She could ruin that woman. Was she justified in doing so?

Clare had always held herself aloof from the backbiting and scandal which is an inevitable part of village life. She hated to feel that she now resembled one of those human ghouls she had always professed to despise.

Suddenly the Vicar's words that morning flashed across her mind:

'*Even to those people their hour comes.*'

Was this *her* hour? Was this *her* temptation? Had it come insidiously disguised as a duty? She was Clare Halliwell, a Christian, in love and charity with all men – and women. If she were to tell Gerald, she must be quite sure that only impersonal motives guided her. For the present she would say nothing.

She paid her bill for luncheon and drove away, feeling an indescribable lightening of spirit. Indeed, she felt happier than she had done for a long time. She felt glad that she had had the strength to resist temptation, to do nothing mean or unworthy. Just for a second it flashed across her mind that it might be a sense of power that had so lightened her spirits, but she dismissed the idea as fantastic.

III

By Tuesday night she was strengthened in her resolve. The revelation could not come through her. She must keep silence. Her own secret love for Gerald made speech impossible. Rather a high-minded view to take? Perhaps; but it was the only one possible for her.

She arrived at the Grange in her own little car. Sir Gerald's chauffeur was at the front door to drive it round to the garage after she had alighted, as the night was a wet one. He had just driven off when Clare remembered some books which she had borrowed and had brought with her to return. She called out, but the man did not hear her. The butler ran out after the car.

So, for a minute or two, Clare was alone in the hall, close to the door of the drawing-room which the butler had just unlatched prior to announcing her. Those inside the room, however, knew nothing of her arrival, and so it was that Vivien's voice, high pitched – not quite the voice of a lady – rang out clearly and distinctly.

'Oh, we're only waiting for Clare Halliwell. You must know her – lives in the village – supposed to be one of the local belles, but frightfully unattractive really. She tried her best to catch Gerald, but he wasn't having any.

'Oh, yes, darling' – this in answer to a murmured protest from her husband. 'She did – you mayn't be aware of the fact – but she did her very utmost. Poor old Clare! A good sort, but such a dump!'

Clare's face went dead white, her hands, hanging against her sides, clenched themselves in anger such as she had never known before. At that moment she could have murdered Vivien Lee. It was only by a supreme physical effort that she regained control of herself. That, and the half-formed thought that she held it in her power to punish Vivien for those cruel words.

The butler had returned with the books. He opened the door, announced her, and in another moment she was greeting a roomful of people in her usual pleasant manner.

Vivien, exquisitely dressed in some dark wine colour that showed off her white fragility, was particularly affectionate and gushing. They didn't see half enough of Clare. She, Vivien, was going to learn golf, and Clare must come out with her on the links.

Gerald was very attentive and kind. Though he had no suspicion that she had overheard his wife's words, he had some vague idea of making up for them. He was very fond of Clare, and he wished Vivien wouldn't say the things she did. He and Clare had been friends, nothing more – and if there was an uneasy suspicion at the back of his mind that he was shirking the truth in that last statement, he put it away from him.

After dinner the talk fell on dogs, and Clare recounted Rover's accident. She purposely waited for a lull in the conversation to say:

'. . . so, on Saturday, I took him to Skippington.'

She heard the sudden rattle of Vivien Lee's coffee-cup on the saucer, but she did not look at her – yet.

'To see that man, Reeves?'

'Yes. He'll be all right, I think. I had lunch at the *County Arms* afterwards. Rather a decent little pub.' She turned now to Vivien. 'Have you ever stayed there?'

If she had had any doubts, they were swept aside. Vivien's answer came quick – in stammering haste.

'I? Oh! N-no, no.'

Fear was in her eyes. They were wide and dark with it, as they met Clare's. Clare's eyes told nothing. They were calm, scrutinizing. No one could have dreamt of the keen pleasure that they veiled. At that moment Clare almost forgave Vivien for the words she had overheard earlier in the evening. She tasted in that moment a fullness of power that almost made her head reel. She held Vivien Lee in the hollow of her hand.

The following day, she received a note from the other woman. Would Clare come up and have tea with her quietly that afternoon? Clare refused.

Then Vivien called on her. Twice she came at hours when Clare was almost certain to be at home. On the first occasion, Clare really was out; on the second, she slipped out by the back way when she saw Vivien coming up the path.

'She's not sure yet whether I know or not,' she said to herself. 'She wants to find out without committing herself. But she shan't – not until I'm ready.'

Clare hardly knew herself what she was waiting for. She had decided to keep silence – that was the only straight and honourable course. She felt an additional glow of virtue when she remembered the extreme provocation she had received. After overhearing the way Vivien talked of her behind her back, a weaker character, she felt, might have abandoned her good resolutions.

She went twice to church on Sunday. First to early Communion, from which she came out strengthened and uplifted. No personal feelings should weigh with her – nothing mean or petty. She went again to morning service. Mr Wilmot preached on the famous prayer of the Pharisee. He sketched the life of that man, a good man, pillar of the church. And he pictured the slow, creeping blight of spiritual pride that distorted and soiled all that he was.

Clare did not listen very attentively. Vivien was in the big square pew of the Lee family, and Clare knew by instinct that the other intended to get hold of her afterwards.

So it fell out. Vivien attached herself to Clare, walked home with her, and asked if she might come in. Clare, of course, assented. They sat in Clare's little sitting-room, bright with flowers and old-fashioned chintzes. Vivien's talk was desultory and jerky.

'I was at Bournemouth, you know, last weekend,' she remarked presently.

'Gerald told me so,' said Clare.

They looked at each other. Vivien appeared almost plain today. Her face had a sharp, foxy look that robbed it of much of its charm.

'When you were at Skippington –' began Vivien.

'When I was at Skippington?' echoed Clare politely.

'You were speaking about some little hotel there.'

'The *County Arms*. Yes. You didn't know it, you said?'

'I – I have been there once.'

'Oh!'

She had only to keep still and wait. Vivien was quite unfitted to bear a strain of any kind. Already she was

69

breaking down under it. Suddenly she leant forward and spoke vehemently.

'You don't like me. You never have. You've always hated me. You're enjoying yourself now, playing with me like a cat with a mouse. You're cruel – cruel. That's why I'm afraid of you, because deep down you're cruel.'

'Really, Vivien!' said Clare sharply.

'You *know*, don't you? Yes, I can see that you know. You knew that night – when you spoke about Skippington. You've found out somehow. Well, I want to know what you are going to do about it? What are you going to do?'

Clare did not reply for a minute, and Vivien sprang to her feet.

'What are you going to do? I must know. You're not going to deny that you know all about it?'

'I do not propose to deny anything,' said Clare coldly.

'You saw me there that day?'

'No. I saw your handwriting in the book – Mr and Mrs Cyril Brown.'

Vivien flushed darkly.

'Since then,' continued Clare quietly, 'I have made inquiries. I find that you were not at Bournemouth that weekend. Your mother never sent for you. Exactly the same thing happened about six weeks previously.'

Vivien sank down again on the sofa. She burst into furious crying, the crying of a frightened child.

'What are you going to do?' she gasped. 'Are you going to tell Gerald?'

'I don't know yet,' said Clare.

She felt calm, omnipotent.

Vivien sat up, pushing the red curls back from her forehead.

'Would you like to hear all about it?'

'It would be as well, I think.'

Vivien poured out the whole story. There was no reticence in her. Cyril 'Brown' was Cyril Haviland, a young engineer to whom she had previously been engaged. His health failed, and he lost his job, whereupon he made no bones about jilting the penniless Vivien and marrying a rich widow many years older than himself. Soon afterwards Vivien married Gerald Lee.

She had met Cyril again by chance. That was the first of many meetings. Cyril, backed by his wife's money, was prospering in his career, and becoming a well-known figure. It was a sordid story, a story of backstairs meeting, of ceaseless lying and intrigue.

'I love him so,' Vivien repeated again and again, with a sudden moan, and each time the words made Clare feel physically sick.

At last the stammering recital came to an end. Vivien muttered a shamefaced: 'Well?'

71

'What am I going to do?' asked Clare. 'I can't tell you. I must have time to think.'

'You won't give me away to Gerald?'

'It may be my duty to do so.'

'No, no.' Vivien's voice rose to a hysterical shriek. 'He'll divorce me. He won't listen to a word. He'll find out from that hotel, and Cyril will be dragged into it. And then his wife will divorce him. Everything will go – his career, his health – he'll be penniless again. He'd never forgive me – never.'

'If you'll excuse my saying so,' said Clare, 'I don't think much of this Cyril of yours.'

Vivien paid no attention.

'I tell you he'll hate me – hate me. I can't bear it. Don't tell Gerald. I'll do anything you like, but don't tell Gerald.'

'I must have time to decide,' said Clare gravely. 'I can't promise anything off-hand. In the meantime, you and Cyril mustn't meet again.'

'No, no, we won't. I swear it.'

'When I know what's the right thing to do,' said Clare, 'I'll let you know.'

She got up. Vivien went out of the house in a furtive, slinking way, glancing back over her shoulder.

Clare wrinkled her nose in disgust. A beastly affair. Would Vivien keep her promise not to see Cyril? Probably not. She was weak – rotten all through.

That afternoon Clare went for a long walk. There was a path which led along the downs. On the left the green hills sloped gently down to the sea far below, while the path wound steadily upward. This walk was known locally as the Edge. Though safe enough if you kept to the path, it was dangerous to wander from it. Those insidious gentle slopes were dangerous. Clare had lost a dog there once. The animal had gone racing over the smooth grass, gaining momentum, had been unable to stop and had gone over the edge of the cliff to be dashed to pieces on the sharp rocks below.

The afternoon was clear and beautiful. From far below there came the ripple of the sea, a soothing murmur. Clare sat down on the short green turf and stared out over the blue water. She must face this thing clearly. What did she mean to do?

She thought of Vivien with a kind of disgust. How the girl had crumpled up, how abjectly she had surrendered! Clare felt a rising contempt. She had no pluck – no grit.

Nevertheless, much as she disliked Vivien, Clare decided that she would continue to spare her for the present. When she got home she wrote a note to her, saying that although she could make no definite promise for the future, she had decided to keep silence for the present.

Life went on much the same in Daymer's End. It was

noticed locally that Lady Lee was looking far from well. On the other hand, Clare Halliwell bloomed. Her eyes were brighter, she carried her head higher, and there was a new confidence and assurance in her manner. She and Lady Lee often met, and it was noticed on these occasions that the younger woman watched the older with a flattering attention to her slightest word.

Sometimes Miss Halliwell would make remarks that seemed a little ambiguous – not entirely relevant to the matter in hand. She would suddenly say that she had changed her mind about many things lately – that it was curious how a little thing might alter one's point of view entirely. One was apt to give way too much to pity – and that was really quite wrong.

When she said things of that kind she usually looked at Lady Lee in a peculiar way, and the latter would suddenly grow quite white, and look almost terrified.

But as the year drew on, these little subtleties became less apparent. Clare continued to make the same remarks, but Lady Lee seemed less affected by them. She began to recover her looks and spirits. Her old gay manner returned.

IV

One morning, when she was taking her dog for a walk, Clare met Gerald in a lane. The latter's spaniel fraternized with Rover, while his master talked to Clare.

'Heard our news?' he said buoyantly. 'I expect Vivien's told you.'

'What sort of news? Vivien hasn't mentioned anything in particular.'

'We're going abroad – for a year – perhaps longer. Vivien's fed up with this place. She never has cared for it, you know.' He sighed, for a moment or two he looked downcast. Gerald Lee was very proud of his home. 'Anyway, I've promised her a change. I've taken a villa near Algiers. A wonderful place, by all accounts.' He laughed a little self-consciously. 'Quite a second honeymoon, eh?'

For a minute or two Clare could not speak. Something seemed rising up in her throat and suffocating her. She could see the white walls of the villa, the orange trees, smell the soft perfumed breath of the South. A second honeymoon!

They were going to escape. Vivien no longer believed in her threats. She was going away, care-free, gay, happy.

Clare heard her own voice, a little hoarse in timbre,

75

saying the appropriate things. How lovely! She envied them!

Mercifully at that moment Rover and the spaniel decided to disagree. In the scuffle that ensued further conversation was out of the question.

That afternoon Clare sat down and wrote a note to Vivien. She asked her to meet her on the Edge the following day, as she had something very important to say to her.

V

The next morning dawned bright and cloudless. Clare walked up the steep path of the Edge with a lightened heart. What a perfect day! She was glad that she had decided to say what had to be said out in the open, under the blue sky, instead of in her stuffy little sitting-room. She was sorry for Vivien, very sorry indeed, but the thing had got to be done.

She saw a yellow dot, like some yellow flower higher up by the side of the path. As she came nearer it resolved itself into the figure of Vivien, dressed in a yellow knitted frock, sitting on the short turf, her hands clasped round her knees.

'Good morning,' said Clare. 'Isn't it a perfect morning?'

'Is it?' said Vivien. 'I haven't noticed. What was it you wanted to say to me?'

Clare dropped down on the grass beside her.

'I'm quite out of breath,' she said apologetically. 'It's a steep pull up here.'

'Damn you!' cried Vivien shrilly. 'Why can't you say it, you smooth-faced devil, instead of torturing me?'

Clare looked shocked, and Vivien hastily recanted.

'I didn't mean that. I'm sorry, Clare. I am indeed. Only – my nerves are all to pieces, and your sitting here and talking about the weather – well, it got me all rattled.'

'You'll have a nervous breakdown if you're not careful,' said Clare coldly.

Vivien gave a short laugh.

'Go over the edge? No – I'm not that kind. I'll never be a loony. Now tell me – what's all this about?'

Clare was silent for a moment, then she spoke, looking not at Vivien, but steadily out over the sea.

'I thought it only fair to warn you that I can no longer keep silence about – about what happened last year.'

'You mean – you'll go to Gerald with the whole story?'

'Unless you'll tell him yourself. That would be infinitely the better way.'

Vivien laughed sharply.

'You know well enough I haven't got the pluck to do that.'

Clare did not contradict the assertion. She had had proof before of Vivien's utterly craven temper.

'It would be infinitely better,' she repeated.

Again Vivien gave that short, ugly laugh.

'It's your precious conscience, I suppose, that drives you to do this?' she sneered.

'I dare say it seems very strange to you,' said Clare quietly. 'But it honestly is that.'

Vivien's white, set face stared into hers.

'My God!' she said. 'I really believe you mean it, too. You actually think that's the reason.'

'It *is* the reason.'

'No, it isn't. If so, you'd have done it before – long ago. Why didn't you? No, don't answer. I'll tell you. You got more pleasure out of holding it over me – that's why. You liked to keep me on tenterhooks, and make me wince and squirm. You'd say things – diabolical things – just to torment me and keep me perpetually on the jump. And so they did for a bit – till I got used to them.'

'You got to feel secure,' said Clare.

'You saw that, didn't you? But even then, you held back, enjoying your sense of power. But now we're going away, escaping from you, perhaps even going to be happy – you couldn't stick that at any price. So your convenient conscience wakes up!'

She stopped, panting. Clare said, still very quietly:

'I can't prevent your saying all these fantastical things; but I can assure you they're not true.'

Vivien turned suddenly and caught her by the hand.

'Clare – for God's sake! I've been straight – I've done what you said. I've not seen Cyril again – I swear it.'

'That's nothing to do with it.'

'Clare – haven't you any pity – any kindness? I'll go down on my knees to you.'

'Tell Gerald yourself. If you tell him, he may forgive you.'

Vivien laughed scornfully.

'You know Gerald better than that. He'll be rabid – vindictive. He'll make me suffer – he'll make Cyril suffer. That's what I can't bear. Listen, Clare – he's doing so well. He's invented something – machinery, I don't understand about it, but it may be a wonderful success. He's working it out now – his wife supplies the money for it, of course. But she's suspicious – jealous. If she finds out, and she will find out if Gerald starts proceedings for divorce – she'll chuck Cyril – his work, everything. Cyril will be ruined.'

'I'm not thinking of Cyril,' said Clare. 'I'm thinking of Gerald. Why don't you think a little of him, too?'

'Gerald! I don't care that –' she snapped her fingers

'for Gerald. I never have. We might as well have the truth now we're at it. But I do care for Cyril. I'm a rotter, through and through, I admit it. I dare say he's a rotter, too. But my feeling for him – that *isn't* rotten. I'd die for him, do you hear? I'd die for him!'

'That is easily said,' said Clare derisively.

'You think I'm not in earnest? Listen, if you go on with this beastly business, I'll kill myself. Sooner than have Cyril brought into it and ruined, I'd do that.'

Clare remained unimpressed.

'You don't believe me?' said Vivien, panting.

'Suicide needs a lot of courage.'

Vivien flinched back as though she had been struck.

'You've got me there. Yes, I've no pluck. If there were an easy way –'

'There's an easy way in front of you,' said Clare. 'You've only got to run straight down that green slope. It would be all over in a couple of minutes. Remember that child last year.'

'Yes,' said Vivien thoughtfully. 'That would be easy – quite easy – if one really wanted to –'

Clare laughed.

Vivien turned to her.

'Let's have this out once more. Can't you see that by keeping silence as long as you have, you've – you've no right to go back on it now? I'll not see Cyril again.

I'll be a good wife to Gerald – I swear I will. Or I'll go away and never see him again? Whichever you like. Clare –'

Clare got up.

'I advise you,' she said, 'to tell your husband yourself . . . otherwise – I shall.'

'I see,' said Vivien softly. 'Well, I can't let Cyril suffer . . .'

She got up, stood still as though considering for a minute or two, then ran lightly down to the path, but instead of stopping, crossed it and went down the slope. Once she half turned her head and waved a hand gaily to Clare, then she ran on gaily, lightly, as a child might run, out of sight . . .

Clare stood petrified. Suddenly she heard cries, shouts, a clamour of voices. Then – silence.

She picked her way stiffly down to the path. About a hundred yards away a party of people coming up it had stopped. They were staring and pointing. Clare ran down and joined them.

'Yes, Miss, someone's fallen over the cliff. Two men have gone down – to see.'

She waited. Was it an hour, or eternity, or only a few minutes?

A man came toiling up the ascent. It was the Vicar in his shirt sleeves. His coat had been taken off to cover what lay below.

'Horrible,' he said, his face was very white. 'Mercifully death must have been instantaneous.'

He saw Clare, and came over to her.

'This must have been a terrible shock to you. You were taking a walk together, I understand?'

Clare heard herself answering mechanically.

Yes. They had just parted. No, Lady Lee's manner had been quite normal. One of the group interposed the information that the lady was laughing and waving her hand. A terribly dangerous place – there ought to be a railing along the path.

The Vicar's voice rose again.

'An accident – yes, clearly an accident.'

And then suddenly Clare laughed – a hoarse, raucous laugh that echoed along the cliff.

'*That's a damned lie*,' she said. '*I killed her.*'

She felt someone patting her shoulder, a voice spoke soothingly.

'There, there. It's all right. You'll be all right presently.'

VI

But Clare was not all right presently. She was never all right again. She persisted in the delusion – certainly a delusion, since at least eight persons had witnessed the scene – that she had killed Vivien Lee.

She was very miserable till Nurse Lauriston came to take charge. Nurse Lauriston was very successful with mental cases.

'Humour them, poor things,' she would say comfortably.

So she told Clare that she was a wardress from Pentonville Prison. Clare's sentence, she said, had been commuted to penal servitude for life. A room was fitted up as a cell.

'And now, I think, we shall be quite happy and comfortable,' said Nurse Lauriston to the doctor. 'Round-bladed knives if you like, doctor, but I don't think there's the least fear of suicide. She's not the type. Too self-centred. Funny how those are often the ones who go over the edge most easily.'

Afterword

'The Edge' was first published in *Pearson's Magazine* in February 1927, with the suggestive editorial comment that the story was 'written just before this author's recent illness and mysterious disappearance'. Late on the evening of 3 December 1926, Agatha Christie left her home in Berkshire. Early on the morning of the following day, her car was found, empty, at Newlands Corner near Shere in Surrey. Policemen and volunteers searched the countryside in vain, but a week and a half elapsed before various members of staff at a hotel in Harrogate realized that the guest who had registered under the name of Theresa Neele was in fact the missing novelist.

After her return, Christie's husband announced to the press that she had suffered 'the most complete loss of memory', but the circumstances surrounding this comparatively minor event in her life have given rise to some speculation over the years. Even while Christie was missing, Edgar Wallace, the famous writer of thrillers, commented in a newspaper article that, if not dead, she 'must be alive and in full possession of her faculties, probably in London. To put it vulgarly,' Wallace continued, 'her first intention seems to have been to "spite" an unknown person.' Neele was the surname of the woman who went on to become the second wife of Archibald Christie and it has been suggested that, after abandoning her car in order to embarrass her husband, Christie spent the night of 3 December with friends in London before travelling to Harrogate. It has even been suggested that the disappearance was staged as some kind of bizarre publicity stunt. Nevertheless, although some aspects of the incident remain unclear, there is nothing to substantiate any of these various alternative 'explanations' which therefore are little more than idle speculation.

Christmas Adventure

I

The big logs crackled merrily in the wide, open fire-place, and above their crackling rose the babel of six tongues all wagging industriously together. The house-party of young people were enjoying their Christmas.

Old Miss Endicott, known to most of those present as Aunt Emily, smiled indulgently on the clatter.

'Bet you you can't eat six mince-pies, Jean.'

'Yes, I can.'

'No, you can't.'

'You'll get the pig out of the trifle if you do.'

'Yes, *and* three helps of trifle, *and* two helps of plum-pudding.'

'I hope the pudding will be good,' said Miss Endicott apprehensively. 'But they were only made three days ago. Christmas puddings ought to be made a long time before Christmas. Why, I remember when I was a child, I thought the last Collect before Advent – "Stir up, O Lord, we beseech Thee . . ." – referred in some way to stirring up the Christmas puddings!'

There was a polite pause while Miss Endicott was speaking. Not because any of the young people were in the least interested in her reminiscences of bygone days, but because they felt that some show of attention was due by good manners to their hostess. As soon as she stopped, the babel burst out again. Miss Endicott sighed, and glanced towards the only member of the party whose years approached her own, as though in search of sympathy – a little man with a curious egg-shaped head and fierce upstanding moustaches. Young people were not what they were, reflected Miss Endicott. In olden days there would have been a mute, respectful circle, listening to the pearls of wisdom dropped by their elders. Instead of which there was all this nonsensical chatter, most of it utterly incomprehensible. All the same, they were dear children! Her eyes softened as she passed them in review – tall, freckled Jean; little Nancy Cardell, with her dark, gipsy beauty; the two younger boys home from school, Johnnie and Eric, and their friend, Charlie Pease; and fair, beautiful Evelyn Haworth . . . At thought of the last, her brow contracted a little, and her eyes wandered to where her eldest nephew, Roger, sat morosely silent, taking no part in the fun, with his eyes fixed on the exquisite Northern fairness of the young girl.

'Isn't the snow ripping?' cried Johnnie, approaching the window. 'Real Christmas weather. I say, let's have a snowball fight. There's lots of time before dinner, isn't there, Aunt Emily?'

'Yes, my dear. We have it at two o'clock. That reminds me, I had better see to the table.'

She hurried out of the room.

'I tell you what. We'll make a snowman!' screamed Jean.

'Yes, what fun! I know; we'll do a snow statue of M. Poirot. Do you hear, M. Poirot? The great detective, Hercule Poirot, modelled in snow, by six celebrated artists!'

The little man in the chair bowed his acknowledgements with a twinkling eye.

'Make him very handsome, my children,' he urged. 'I insist on that.'

'Ra-ther!'

The troop disappeared like a whirlwind, colliding in the doorway with a stately butler who was entering with a note on a salver. The butler, his calm re-established, advanced towards Poirot.

Poirot took the note and tore it open. The butler departed. Twice the little man read the note through, then he folded it up and put it in his pocket. Not a muscle of his face had moved, and yet the contents of the note were sufficiently surprising. Scrawled in an illiterate hand were the words: '*Don't eat any plum-pudding.*'

'Very interesting,' murmured M. Poirot to himself. 'And quite unexpected.'

He looked across to the fireplace. Evelyn Haworth had not gone out with the rest. She was sitting staring at the fire, absorbed in thought, nervously twisting a ring on the third finger of her left hand round and round.

'You are lost in a dream, Mademoiselle,' said the little man at last. 'And the dream is not a happy one, eh?'

She started, and looked across at him uncertainly. He nodded reassuringly.

'It is my business to know things. No, you are not happy. Me, too, I am not very happy. Shall we confide in each other? See you, I have the big sorrow because a friend of mine, a friend of many years, has gone away across the sea to the South America. Sometimes, when we were together, this friend made me impatient, his stupidity enraged me; but now that he is gone, I can remember only his good qualities. That is the way of life, is it not? And now, Mademoiselle, what is your trouble? You are not like me, old and alone – you are young and beautiful; and the man you love loves you – oh yes, it is so: I have been watching him for the last half-hour.'

The girl's colour rose.

'You mean Roger Endicott? Oh, but you have made a mistake; it is not Roger I am engaged to.'

'No, you are engaged to Mr Oscar Levering. I know that perfectly. But why are you engaged to him, since you love another man?'

The girl did not seem to resent his words; indeed, there was something in his manner which made that impossible. He spoke with a mixture of kindliness and authority that was irresistible.

'Tell me all about it,' said Poirot gently; and he added the phrase he had used before, the sound of which was oddly comforting to the girl. 'It is my business to know things.'

'I am so miserable, M. Poirot – so very miserable. You see, once we were very well off. I was supposed to be an heiress, and Roger was only a younger son; and – and although I'm sure he cared for me, he never said anything, but went off to Australia.'

'It is droll, the way they arrange the marriages over here,' interpolated M. Poirot. 'No order. No method. Everything left to chance.'

Evelyn continued.

'Then suddenly we lost all our money. My mother and I were left almost penniless. We moved into a tiny house, and we could just manage. But my mother became very ill. The only chance for her was to have a serious operation and go abroad to a warm climate.

91

And we hadn't the money, M. Poirot – we hadn't the money! It meant that she must die. Mr Levering had proposed to me once or twice already. He again asked me to marry him, and promised to do everything that could be done for my mother. I said yes – what else could I do? He kept his word. The operation was performed by the greatest specialist of the day, and we went to Egypt for the winter. That was a year ago. My mother is well and strong again; and I – I am to marry Mr Levering after Christmas.'

'I see,' said M. Poirot; 'and in the meantime, M. Roger's elder brother has died, and he has come home – to find his dream shattered. All the same, you are not yet married, Mademoiselle.'

'A Haworth does not break her word, M. Poirot,' said the girl proudly.

Almost as she spoke, the door opened, and a big man with a rubicund face, narrow, crafty eyes, and a bald head stood on the threshold.

'What are you moping in here for, Evelyn? Come out for a stroll.'

'Very well, Oscar.'

She rose listlessly. Poirot rose also and demanded politely:

'Mademoiselle Levering, she is still indisposed?'

'Yes, I'm sorry to say my sister is still in bed. Too bad, to be laid up on Christmas Day.'

'It is indeed,' agreed the detective politely.

A few minutes sufficed for Evelyn to put on her snow-boots and some wraps, and she and her fiancé went out into the snow-covered grounds. It was an ideal Christmas Day, crisp and sunny. The rest of the house-party were busy with the erection of the snowman. Levering and Evelyn paused to watch them.

'Love's young dream, yah!' cried Johnnie, and threw a snowball at them.

'What do you think of it, Evelyn?' cried Jean. 'M. Hercule Poirot, the great detective.'

'Wait till the moustache goes on,' said Eric. 'Nancy's going to clip off a bit of her hair for it. *Vivent les braves Belges!* Pom, pom!'

'Fancy having a real-live detective in the house!' – this from Charlie – 'I wish there could be a murder, too.'

'Oh, oh, oh!' cried Jean, dancing about. 'I've got an idea. Let's get up a murder – a spoof one, I mean. And take him in. Oh, do let's – it would be no end of a rag.'

Five voices began to talk at once.

'How should we do it?'

'Awful groans!'

'No, you stupid, out here.'

'Footprints in the snow, of course.'

'Jean in her nightie.'

'You do it with red paint.'

'In your hand – and clap it to your head.'

'I say, I wish we had a revolver.'

'I tell you, Father and Aunt Em won't hear. Their rooms are the other side of the house.'

'No, he won't mind a bit; he's no end of a sport.'

'Yes, but what kind of red paint? Enamel?'

'We could get some in the village.'

'Fat-head, not on Christmas Day.'

'No, watercolour. Crimson lake.'

'Jean can be it.'

'Never mind if you *are* cold. It won't be for long.'

'No, Nancy can be it, Nancy's got those posh pyjamas.'

'Let's see if Graves knows where there's any paint.'

A stampede to the house.

'In a brown study, Endicott?' said Levering, laughing disagreeably.

Roger roused himself abruptly. He had heard little of what had passed.

'I was just wondering,' he said quietly.

'Wondering?'

'Wondering what M. Poirot was doing down here at all.'

Levering seemed taken aback; but at that moment the big gong pealed out, and everybody went in to Christmas dinner. The curtains were drawn in the dining-room, and the lights on, illuminating the long table piled high with crackers and other decorations. It was a real old-fashioned Christmas dinner. At one end of the table was the Squire, red-faced and jovial; his sister faced him at the other. M. Poirot, in honour of the occasion, had donned a red waistcoat, and his plumpness, and the way he carried his head on one side, reminded one irresistibly of a robin redbreast.

The Squire carved rapidly, and everyone fell to on turkey. The carcasses of two turkeys were removed, and there fell a breathless hush. Then Graves, the butler, appeared in state, bearing the plum-pudding aloft – a gigantic pudding wreathed in flames. A hullabaloo broke out.

'Quick. Oh! my piece is going out. Buck up, Graves; unless it's still burning, I shan't get my wish.'

Nobody had leisure to notice a curious expression on the face of M. Poirot as he surveyed the portion of pudding on his plate. Nobody observed the lightning glance he sent round the table. With a faint, puzzled frown he began to eat his pudding. Everybody began to eat pudding. The conversation was more subdued. Suddenly the Squire uttered an exclamation. His face became purple and his hand went to his mouth.

'Confound it, Emily!' he roared. 'Why do you let the cook put glass in the puddings?'

'Glass?' cried Miss Endicott, astonished.

The Squire withdrew the offending substance from his mouth.

'Might have broken a tooth,' he grumbled. 'Or swallowed it and had appendicitis.'

In front of each person was a small finger-bowl of water, designed to receive the sixpences and other matters found in the trifle. Mr Endicott dropped the piece of glass into this, rinsed it and held it up.

'God bless my soul!' he ejaculated. 'It's a red stone out of one of the cracker brooches.'

'You permit?' Very deftly, M. Poirot took it from his fingers and examined it attentively. As the Squire had said, it was a big red stone, the colour of a ruby. The light gleamed from its facets as he turned it about.

'Gee!' cried Eric. 'Suppose it's real.'

'Silly boy!' said Jean scornfully. 'A ruby that size would be worth thousands and thousands and thousands – wouldn't it, M. Poirot?'

'Extraordinary how well they get up these cracker things,' murmured Miss Endicott. '*But how did it get into the pudding?*'

Undoubtedly that was the question of the hour. Every hypothesis was exhausted. Only M. Poirot said nothing, but carelessly, as though thinking of something else, he dropped the stone into his pocket.

After dinner he paid a visit to the kitchen.

The cook was rather flustered. To be questioned by a

member of the house-party, and the foreign gentleman too! But she did her best to answer his questions. The puddings had been made three days ago – 'The day you arrived, Sir.' Everyone had come out into the kitchen to have a stir and wish. An old custom – perhaps they didn't have it abroad? After that the puddings were boiled, and then they were put in a row on the top shelf in the larder. Was there anything special to distinguish this pudding from the others? No, she didn't think so. Except that it was in an aluminium pudding-basin, and the others were in china ones. Was it the pudding originally intended for Christmas Day? It was funny that he should ask that. No, indeed! The Christmas pudding was always boiled in a big white china mould with a pattern of holly-leaves. But this very morning (the cook's red face became wrathful) Gladys, the kitchen-maid, sent to fetch it down for the final boiling, had managed to drop and break it. 'And of course, seeing that there might be splinters in it, I wouldn't send it to table, but took the big aluminium one instead.'

M. Poirot thanked her for her information. He went out of the kitchen, smiling a little to himself, as though satisfied with the information he had obtained. And the fingers of his right hand played with something in his pocket.

II

'M. Poirot! M. Poirot! Do wake up! Something dreadful's happened!'

Thus Johnnie in the early hours of the following morning. M. Poirot sat up in bed. He wore a night-cap. The contrast between the dignity of his countenance and the rakish tilt of the night-cap was certainly droll; but its effect on Johnnie seemed disproportionate. But for his words, one might have fancied that the boy was violently amused about something. Curious sounds came from outside the door, too, suggesting soda-water syphons in difficulty.

'Come down at once, please,' continued Johnnie, his voice shaking slightly. 'Someone's been killed.' He turned away.

'Aha, that is serious!' said M. Poirot.

He arose, and, without unduly hurrying himself, made a partial toilet. Then he followed Johnnie down the stairs. The house-party was clustered round the door into the garden. Their countenances all expressed intense emotion. At sight of him Eric was seized with a violent choking fit.

Jean came forward and laid her hand on M. Poirot's arm.

'Look!' she said, and pointed dramatically through the open door.

'*Mon Dieu!*' ejaculated M. Poirot. 'It is like a scene on the stage.'

His remark was not inapposite. More snow had fallen during the night, the world looked white and ghostly in the faint light of the early dawn. The expanse of white lay unbroken save for what looked like on splash of vivid scarlet.

Nancy Cardell lay motionless on the snow. She was clad in scarlet silk pyjamas, her small feet were bare, her arms were spread wide. Her head was turned aside and hidden by the mass of her clustering black hair. Deadly still she lay, and from her left side rose up the hilt of a dagger, whilst on the snow there was an ever-widening patch of crimson.

Poirot went out into the snow. He did not go to where the girl's body lay, but kept to the path. Two tracks of foot-marks, a man's and a woman's, led to where the tragedy had occurred. The man's footprints went away in the opposite direction alone. Poirot stood on the path, stroking his chin reflectively.

Suddenly Oscar Levering burst out of the house.

'Good God!' he cried. 'What's this?'

His excitement was a contrast to the other's calm.

'It looks,' said M. Poirot thoughtfully, 'like murder.'

Eric had another violent attack of coughing.

'But we must do something,' cried the other. 'What shall we do?'

'There is only one thing to be done,' said M. Poirot. 'Send for the police.'

'Oh!' said everybody at once.

M. Poirot looked inquiringly at them.

'Certainly,' he said. 'It is the only thing to be done. Who will go?'

There was a pause, then Johnnie came forward.

'Rag's over,' he declared. 'I say, M. Poirot, I hope you won't be too mad with us. It's all a joke, you know – got up between us – just to pull your leg. Nancy's only shamming.'

M. Poirot regarded him without visible emotion, save that his eyes twinkled a moment.

'You mock yourselves at me, is that it?' he inquired placidly.

'I say, I'm awfully sorry really. We shouldn't have done it. Beastly bad taste. I apologize, I really do.'

'You need not apologize,' said the other in a peculiar voice.

Johnnie turned.

'I say, Nancy, get up!' he cried. 'Don't lie there all day.'

But the figure on the ground did not move.

'Get up,' cried Johnnie again.

Still Nancy did not move, and suddenly a feeling

of nameless dread came over the boy. He turned to Poirot.

'What – what's the matter? Why doesn't she get up?'

'Come with me,' said Poirot curtly.

He strode over the snow. He had waved the others back, and he was careful not to infringe on the other footmarks. The boy followed him, frightened and unbelieving. Poirot knelt down by the girl, then he signed to Johnnie.

'Feel her hand and pulse.'

Wondering, the boy bent down, then started back with a cry. The hand and arm were stiff and cold, and no vestige of a pulse was to be found.

'She's dead!' he gasped. 'But how? Why?'

M. Poirot passed over the first part of the question.

'Why?' he said musingly. 'I wonder.' Then, suddenly leaning across the dead girl's body, he unclasped her other hand, which was tightly clenched over something. Both he and the boy uttered an exclamation. In the palm of Nancy's hand was a red stone that winked and flashed forth fire.

'Aha!' cried M. Poirot. Swift as a flash his hand flew to his pocket, and came away empty.

'The cracker ruby,' said Johnnie wonderingly. Then, as his companion bent to examine the dagger, and the stained snow, he cried out: 'Surely it can't be blood, M. Poirot. It's paint. It's only paint.'

Poirot straightened himself.

'Yes,' he said quietly. 'You are right. It's only paint.'

'Then how –' The boy broke off. Poirot finished the sentence for him.

'How was she killed? That we must find out. Did she eat or drink anything this morning?'

He was retracing his steps to the path where the others waited as he spoke. Johnnie was close behind him.

'She had a cup of tea,' said the boy. 'Mr Levering made it for her. He's got a spirit-lamp in his room.'

Johnnie's voice was loud and clear. Levering heard the words.

'Always take a spirit-lamp about with me,' he declared. 'Most handy thing in the world. My sister's been glad enough of it this visit – not liking to worry the servants all the time you know.'

M. Poirot's eyes fell, almost apologetically as it seemed, to Mr Levering's feet, which were encased in carpet slippers.

'You have changed your boots, I see,' he murmured gently.

Levering stared at him.

'But, M. Poirot,' cried Jean, 'what are we to do?'

'There is only one thing to be done, as I said just now, Mademoiselle. Send for the police.'

'I'll go,' cried Levering. 'It won't take me a minute

to put on my boots. You people had better not stay
out here in the cold.'

He disappeared into the house.

'He is so thoughtful, that Mr Levering,' murmured
Poirot softly. 'Shall we take his advice?'

'What about waking father and – and everybody?'

'No,' said M. Poirot sharply. 'It is quite unnecessary.
Until the police come, nothing must be touched out
here; so shall we go inside? To the library? I have a
little history to recount to you which may distract your
minds from this sad tragedy.'

He led the way, and they followed him.

'The story is about a ruby,' said M. Poirot, ensconcing
himself in a comfortable arm-chair. 'A very celebrated
ruby which belonged to a very celebrated man. I will
not tell you his name – but he is one of the great ones of
the earth. *Eh bien*, this great man, he arrived in London,
incognito. And since, though a great man, he was also
a young and a foolish man, he became entangled with
a pretty young lady. The pretty young lady, she did
not care much for the man, but she did care for his
possessions – so much so that she disappeared one
day with the historic ruby which had belonged to his
house for generations. The poor young man, he was
in a quandary. He is shortly to be married to a noble
Princess, and he does not want the scandal. Impossible
to go to the police, he comes to me, Hercule Poirot,

instead. "Recover for me my ruby," he says. *Eh bien*, I know something of this young lady. She has a brother, and between them they have put through many a clever *coup*. I happen to know where they are staying for Christmas. By the kindness of Mr Endicott, whom I chance to have met, I, too, become a guest. But when this pretty young lady hears that I am arriving, she is greatly alarmed. She is intelligent, and she knows that I am after the ruby. She must hide it immediately in a safe place; and figure to yourself where she hides it – in a plum-pudding! Yes, you may well say, oh! She is stirring with the rest, you see, and she pops it into a pudding-bowl of aluminium that is different from the others. By a strange chance, that pudding came to be used on Christmas Day.'

The tragedy forgotten for the moment, they stared at him open-mouthed.

'After that,' continued the little man, 'she took to her bed.' He drew out his watch and looked at it. 'The household is astir. Mr Levering is a long time fetching the police, is he not? I fancy that his sister went with him.'

Evelyn rose with a cry, her eyes fixed on Poirot.

'And I also fancy that they will not return. Oscar Levering has been sailing close to the wind for a long time, and this is the end. He and his sister will pursue their activities abroad for a time under a different name. I alternately tempted and frightened him this morning. By casting aside all pretence he could gain possession of the ruby whilst we were in the house and he was supposed to be fetching the police. But it meant burning his boats. Still, with a case being built up against him for murder, flight seemed clearly indicated.'

'Did he kill Nancy?' whispered Jean.

Poirot rose.

'Supposing we visit once more the scene of the crime,' he suggested.

He led the way, and they followed him. But a simultaneous gasp broke from their lips as they passed outside the house. No trace of the tragedy remained; the snow was smooth and unbroken.

'Crikey!' said Eric, sinking down on the step. 'It wasn't all a dream, was it?'

'Most extraordinary,' said M. Poirot, 'The Mystery of the Disappearing Body.' His eyes twinkled gently.

Jean came up to him in sudden suspicion.

'M. Poirot, you haven't – you aren't – I say, you haven't been spoofing us all the time, have you? Oh, I do believe you have!'

'It is true, my children. I knew about your little plot, you see, and I arranged a little counterplot of my own. Ah, here is Mlle. Nancy – and none the worse, I hope, after her magnificent acting of the comedy.'

It was indeed Nancy Cardell in the flesh, her eyes shining and her whole person exuberant with health and vigour.

'You have not caught cold? You drank the tisane I sent to your room?' demanded Poirot accusingly.

'I took one sip and that was enough. I'm all right. Did I do it well, M. Poirot? Oh, my arm hurts after that tourniquet!'

'You were splendid, *petite*. But shall we explain to the others? They are still in the fog, I perceive. See you, *mes enfants*, I went to Mlle. Nancy, told her that I knew all about your little *complot*, and asked her if she would act a part for me. She did it very cleverly. She induced Mr Levering to make her a cup of tea, and also managed that he should be the one chosen to leave footprints on the snow. So when the time came, and he thought that by some fatality she was really dead, I had all the materials to frighten him with. What happened after we went into the house, Mademoiselle?'

'He came down with his sister, snatched the ruby out of my hand, and off they went post-haste.'

'But I say, M. Poirot, what about the ruby?' cried Eric. 'Do you mean to say you've let them have that?'

Poirot's face fell, as he faced a circle of accusing eyes.

'I shall recover it yet,' he said feebly; but he perceived that he had gone down in their estimation.

'Well, I do think!' began Johnnie. 'To let them get away with the ruby –'

But Jean was sharper.

'He's spoofing us again!' she cried. 'You are, aren't you?'

'Feel in my left-hand pocket, Mademoiselle.'

Jean thrust in an eager hand, and drew it out again with a squeal of triumph. She held aloft the great ruby in its crimson splendour.

'You see,' explained Poirot, 'the other was a paste replica I brought with me from London.'

'Isn't he clever?' demanded Jean ecstatically.

'There's one thing you haven't told us,' said Johnnie suddenly. 'How did you know about the rag? Did Nancy tell you?'

Poirot shook his head.

'Then how did you know?'

'It is my business to know things,' said M. Poirot, smiling a little as he watched Evelyn Haworth and Roger Endicott walking down the path together.

'Yes, but do tell us. Oh, do, please! *Dear* M. Poirot, please tell us!'

He was surrounded by a circle of flushed, eager faces.

'You really wish that I should solve for you this mystery?'

'*Yes.*'

'I do not think I can.'

'Why not?'

'*Ma foi*, you will be so disappointed.'

'Oh, do tell us! How *did* you know?'

'Well, you see, I was in the library –'

'Yes?'

'And you were discussing your plans just outside – and the library window was open.'

'Is that all?' said Eric in disgust. 'How simple!'

'Is it not?' said M. Poirot, smiling.

'At all events, we know everything now,' said Jean in a satisfied voice.

'Do we?' muttered M. Poirot to himself, as he went into the house. '*I* do not – I, whose business it is to know things.'

And, for perhaps the twentieth time, he drew from his pocket a rather dirty piece of paper.

'Don't eat any plum-pudding –'

M. Poirot shook his head perplexedly. At the same moment he became aware of a peculiar gasping sound very near his feet. He looked down and perceived a small creature in a print dress. In her left hand was a dust-pan, and in the right a brush.

'And who may you be, *mon enfant?*' inquired M. Poirot.

'Annie 'Icks, please, Sir. Between-maid.'

M. Poirot had an inspiration. He handed her the letter.

'Did you write that, Annie?'

'I didn't mean any 'arm, Sir.'

He smiled at her.

'Of course you didn't. Suppose you tell me all about it?'

'It was them two, Sir – Mr Levering and his sister. None of us can abide 'em; and she wasn't ill a bit – we could all tell that. So I thought something queer was going on, and I'll tell you straight, Sir, I listened at the door, and I heard him say as plain as plain, "This fellow Poirot must be got out of the way as soon as possible." And then he says to 'er, meaning-like, "Where did you put it?" And she answers, "In the pudding." And so I saw they meant to poison you in the Christmas pudding, and I didn't know what to do. Cook wouldn't listen to the likes of me. And then I thought of writing a warning, and I put it in the 'all where Mr Graves would be sure to see it and take it to you.'

Annie paused breathless. Poirot surveyed her gravely for some minutes.

'You read too many novelettes, Annie,' he said at last. 'But you have the good heart, and a certain amount of intelligence. When I return to London I will send you an excellent book upon *le ménage*, also the Lives of the Saints, and a work upon the economic position of woman.'

Agatha Christie

Leaving Annie gasping anew, he turned and crossed the hall. He had meant to go into the library, but through the open door he saw a dark head and a fair one, very close together, and he paused where he stood. Suddenly a pair of arms slipped round his neck.

'If you *will* stand just under the mistletoe!' said Jean.

'Me too,' said Nancy.

M. Poirot enjoyed it all – he enjoyed it very much indeed.

Afterword

'Christmas Adventure' was first published as *The Adventure of the Christmas Pudding* in *The Sketch* on 12 December 1923 as the last in the second series of stories published under the heading *The Grey Cells of M. Poirot.* The story reappeared in the 1940s under the title 'Christmas Adventure' in two short-lived collections, *Problem at Pollensa Bay and Christmas Adventure* and *Poirot Knows the Murderer* before, many years later, being extended by Christie to a novella. As such, it was included in *The Adventure of the Christmas Pudding and a Selection of Entrées* (1960).

In the foreword to that collection, Christie described how the story recalled the Christmases of her youth which she and her mother had spent, after her father's death in 1901, at Abney Hall in Stockport. Abney had been built by Sir James Watts, one-time Lord Mayor of Manchester and grandfather of James Watts, the husband of Christie's elder sister, Madge. In her autobiography, published in 1977, Christie described Abney as 'a wonderful house to have Christmas in as a child. Not only was it enormous Victorian Gothic with quantities of rooms, passages, unexpected steps, back staircases, front staircases, alcoves, niches – everything in the world that a child could want – but it also had three different pianos that you could play, as well as an organ.' Elsewhere, she described 'the tables groaning with food and the lavish hospitality . . . there was an open storeroom in which everyone could partake of chocolates and all sorts of delicacies whenever they liked.' And, when Agatha wasn't eating – usually in competition with James Watts' younger brother Humphrey – she was playing with him and his brothers Lionel and Miles and their sister Nan. Perhaps she had them in mind when writing about the children in the story and the fun they had one snowy Christmas with 'a real-live detective in the house'.

The Lonely God

I

He stood on a shelf in the British Museum, alone and forlorn amongst a company of obviously more important deities. Ranged round the four walls, these greater personages all seemed to display an overwhelming sense of their own superiority. The pedestal of each was duly inscribed with the land and race that had been proud to possess him. There was no doubt of their position; they were divinities of importance and recognized as such.

Only the little god in the corner was aloof and remote from their company. Roughly hewn out of grey stone, his features almost totally obliterated by time and exposure, he sat there in isolation, his elbows on his knees, and his head buried in his hands; a lonely little god in a strange country.

There was no inscription to tell the land whence he came. He was indeed lost, without honour or renown, a pathetic little figure very far from home. No one noticed him, no one stopped to look at him. Why should they? He was so insignificant, a block of grey stone in a corner. On either side of him were two Mexican gods worn smooth with age, placid idols with folded hands, and cruel mouths curved in a smile that showed openly their contempt of humanity. There was also a rotund, violently self-assertive little god, with a clenched fist, who evidently suffered from a swollen sense of his own importance, but passers-by stopped to give him a glance sometimes, even if it was only to laugh at the contrast of his absurd pomposity with the smiling indifference of his Mexican companions.

And the little lost god sat on there hopelessly, his head in his hands, as he had sat year in and year out, till one day the impossible happened, and he found – a worshipper.

II

'Any letters for me?'

The hall porter removed a packet of letters from a pigeon-hole, gave a cursory glance through them, and said in a wooden voice:

'Nothing for you, sir.'

Frank Oliver sighed as he walked out of the club again. There was no particular reason why there should have been anything for him. Very few people wrote to him. Ever since he had returned from Burma in the spring, he had become conscious of a growing and increasing loneliness.

Frank Oliver was a man just over forty, and the last eighteen years of his life had been spent in various parts of the globe, with brief furloughs in England. Now that he had retired and come home to live for good, he realized for the first time how very much alone in the world he was.

True, there was his sister Greta, married to a Yorkshire clergyman, very busy with parochial duties and the bringing up of a family of small children. Greta was naturally very fond of her only brother, but equally naturally she had very little time to give him. Then there was his old friend Tom Hurley. Tom was married to a nice, bright, cheerful girl, very energetic and practical, of whom Frank was secretly afraid. She told him brightly that he must not be a crabbed old bachelor, and was always producing 'nice girls'. Frank Oliver found that he never had anything to say to these 'nice girls'; they persevered with him for a while, then gave him up as hopeless.

And yet he was not really unsociable. He had a great longing for companionship and sympathy, and ever since he had been back in England he had become aware of a growing discouragement. He had been away too long, he was out of tune with the times. He spent long, aimless days wandering about, wondering what on earth he was to do with himself next.

It was on one of these days that he strolled into the British Museum. He was interested in Asiatic curiosities, and so it was that he chanced upon the lonely god. Its charm held him at once. Here was something vaguely akin to himself; here, too, was some-one lost and astray in a strange land. He became in the habit of paying frequent visits to the Museum, just to glance in on the little grey stone figure, in its obscure place on the high shelf.

'Rough luck on the little chap,' he thought to himself. 'Probably had a lot of fuss made about him once, kow-towing and offerings and all the rest of it.'

He had begun to feel such a proprietary right in his little friend (it really almost amounted to a sense of actual ownership) that he was inclined to be resentful when he found that the little god had made a second conquest. *He* had discovered the lonely god; nobody else, he felt, had a right to interfere.

But after the first flash of indignation, he was forced to smile at himself. For this second worshipper was such a little bit of a thing, such a ridiculous, pathetic creature, in a shabby black coat and skirt that had seen its best days. She was young, a little over twenty he should judge, with fair hair and blue eyes, and a wistful droop to her mouth.

Her hat especially appealed to his chivalry. She had evidently trimmed it herself, and it made such a brave attempt to be smart that its failure was pathetic. She was obviously a lady, though a poverty-stricken one, and he immediately decided in his own mind that she was a governess and alone in the world.

He soon found out that her days for visiting the god were Tuesdays and Fridays, and she always arrived at ten o'clock, as soon as the Museum was open. At first he disliked her intrusion, but little by little it began to form one of the principal interests of his monotonous life. Indeed, the fellow devotee was fast ousting the object of devotion from his position of pre-eminence. The days that he did not see the 'Little Lonely Lady', as he called her to himself, were blank.

Perhaps she, too, was equally interested in him, though she endeavoured to conceal the fact with studious unconcern. But little by little a sense of fellowship was slowly growing between them, though as yet they had exchanged no spoken word. The truth of the matter was, the man was too shy! He argued to himself that very likely she had not even noticed him (some inner sense gave the lie to that instantly), that she would consider it a great impertinence, and, finally, that he had not the least idea what to say.

But Fate, or the little god, was kind and sent him an inspiration – or what he regarded as such. With infinite delight in his own cunning, he purchased a woman's handkerchief, a frail little affair of cambric and lace which he almost feared to touch, and, thus armed, he followed her as she departed and stopped her in the Egyptian room.

'Excuse me, but is this yours?' He tried to speak with airy unconcern, and signally failed.

The Lonely Lady took it, and made a pretence of examining it with minute care.

'No, it is not mine.' She handed it back, and added, with what he felt guiltily was a suspicious glance: 'It's quite a new one. The price is still on it.'

But he was unwilling to admit that he had been found out. He started on an over-plausible flow of explanation.

'You see, I picked it up under that big case. It was just by the farthest leg of it.' He derived great relief from this detailed account. 'So, as you had been standing there, I thought it must be yours and came after you with it.'

She said again: 'No, it isn't mine,' and added, as if with a sense of ungraciousness, 'thank you.'

The conversation came to an awkward standstill.

The girl stood there, pink and embarrassed, evidently uncertain how to retreat with dignity.

He made a desperate effort to take advantage of his opportunity.

'I – I didn't know there was anyone else in London who cared for our little lonely god till you came.'

She answered eagerly, forgetting her reserve:

'Do *you* call him that too?'

Apparently, if she had noticed his pronoun, she did not resent it. She had been startled into sympathy, and his quiet 'Of course!' seemed the most natural rejoinder in the world.

Again there was a silence, but this time it was a silence born of understanding.

It was the Lonely Lady who broke it in a sudden remembrance of the conventionalities.

She drew herself up to her full height, and with an almost ridiculous assumption of dignity for so small a person, she observed in chilling accents:

'I must be going now. Good morning.' And with a slight, stiff inclination of her head, she walked away, holding herself very erect.

III

By all acknowledged standards Frank Oliver ought to have felt rebuffed, but it is a regrettable sign of his rapid advance in depravity that he merely murmured to himself: 'Little darling!'

He was soon to repent of his temerity, however. For ten days his little lady never came near the Museum. He was in despair! He had frightened her away! She would never come back! He was a brute, a villain! He would never see her again!

In his distress he haunted the British Museum all day long. She might merely have changed her time of coming. He soon began to know the adjacent rooms by heart, and he contracted a lasting hatred of mummies. The guardian policeman observed him with suspicion when he spent three hours poring over Assyrian hieroglyphics, and the contemplation of endless vases of all ages nearly drove him mad with boredom.

But one day his patience was rewarded. She came again, rather pinker than usual, and trying hard to appear self-possessed.

He greeted her with cheerful friendliness.

'Good morning. It is ages since you've been here.'

'Good morning.'

She let the words slip out with icy frigidity, and coldly ignored the end part of his sentence.

But he was desperate.

'Look here!' He stood confronting her with pleading eyes that reminded her irresistibly of a large, faithful dog. 'Won't you be friends? I'm all alone in London – all alone in the world, and I believe you are, too. We ought to be friends. Besides, our little god has introduced us.'

She looked up half doubtfully, but there was a faint smile quivering at the corners of her mouth.

'Has he?'

'Of course!'

It was the second time he had used this extremely positive form of assurance, and now, as before, it did not fail of its effect, for after a minute or two the girl said, in that slightly royal manner of hers:

'Very well.'

'That's splendid,' he replied gruffly, but there was something in his voice as he said it that made the girl glance at him swiftly, with a sharp impulse of pity.

And so the queer friendship began. Twice a week they met, at the shrine of a little heathen idol. At first they confined their conversation solely to him. He was, as it were, at once a palliation of, and an excuse for, their friendship. The question of his origin was widely discussed. The man insisted on attributing to him the

121

most bloodthirsty characteristics. He depicted him as the terror and dread of his native land, insatiable for human sacrifice, and bowed down to by his people in fear and trembling. In the contrast between his former greatness and his present insignificance there lay, according to the man, all the pathos of the situation.

The Lonely Lady would have none of this theory. He was essentially a kind little god, she insisted. She doubted whether he had ever been very powerful. If he had been so, she argued, he would not now be lost and friendless, and, anyway, he was a dear little god, and she loved him, and she hated to think of him sitting there day after day with all those other horrid, supercilious things jeering at him, because you could see they did! After this vehement outburst the little lady was quite out of breath.

That topic exhausted, they naturally began to talk of themselves. He found out that his surmise was correct. She was a nursery governess to a family of children who lived at Hampstead. He conceived an instant dislike of these children; of Ted, who was five and really not *naughty*, only mischievous; of the twins who *were* rather trying, and of Molly, who wouldn't do anything she was told, but was such a dear you couldn't be cross with her!

'Those children bully you,' he said grimly and accusingly to her.

'They do not,' she retorted with spirit. 'I am extremely stern with them.'

'Oh! Ye gods!' he laughed. But she made him apologize humbly for his scepticism.

She was an orphan she told him, quite alone in the world.

Gradually he told her something of his own life: of his official life, which had been painstaking and mildly successful; and of his unofficial pastime, which was the spoiling of yards of canvas.

'Of course, I don't know anything about it,' he explained. 'But I have always felt I could paint something some day. I can sketch pretty decently, but I'd like to do a real picture of something. A chap who knew once told me that my technique wasn't bad.'

She was interested, pressed for details.

'I am sure you paint awfully well.' He shook his head.

'No, I've begun several things lately and chucked them up in despair. I always thought that, when I had the time, it would be plain sailing. I have been storing up that idea for years, but now, like everything else, I suppose, I've left it too late.'

'Nothing's too late – ever,' said the little lady, with the vehement earnestness of the very young.

He smiled down on her. 'You think not, child? It's too late for some things for me.'

123

Agatha Christie

And the little lady laughed at him and nick-named him Methuselah.

They were beginning to feel curiously at home in the British Museum. The solid and sympathetic policeman who patrolled the galleries was a man of tact, and on the appearance of the couple he usually found that his onerous duties of guardianship were urgently needed in the adjoining Assyrian room.

One day the man took a bold step. He invited her out to tea!

At first she demurred.

'I have no time. I am not free. I can come some mornings because the children have French lessons.'

'Nonsense,' said the man. 'You could manage one day. Kill off an aunt or a second cousin or something, but *come*. We'll go to a little ABC shop near here, and have buns for tea! I know you must love buns!'

'Yes, the penny kind with currants!'

'And a lovely glaze on top –'

'They are such plump, dear things –'

'There is something,' Frank Oliver said solemnly, 'infinitely comforting about a bun!'

So it was arranged, and the little governess came, wearing quite an expensive hothouse rose in her belt in honour of the occasion.

He had noticed that, of late, she had a strained, worried look, and it was more apparent than ever this afternoon as she poured out the tea at the little marble-topped table.

'Children been bothering you?' he asked solicitously.

She shook her head. She had seemed curiously disinclined to talk about the children lately.

'*They're* all right. I never mind them.'

'Don't you?'

His sympathetic tone seemed to distress her unwarrantably.

'Oh, no. It was never that. But – but, indeed, I was lonely. I was indeed!' Her tone was almost pleading.

He said quickly, touched: 'Yes, yes, child, I know – I know.'

After a minute's pause he remarked in a cheerful tone: 'Do you know, you haven't even asked my name yet?'

She held up a protesting hand.

'Please, I don't want to know it. And don't ask mine. Let us be just two lonely people who've come together and made friends. It makes it so much more wonderful – and – and different.'

He said slowly and thoughtfully: 'Very well. In an otherwise lonely world we'll be two people who have just each other.'

It was a little different from her way of putting it, and she seemed to find it difficult to go on with the conversation. Instead, she bent lower and lower over her plate, till only the crown of her hat was visible.

'That's rather a nice hat,' he said by way of restoring her equanimity.

'I trimmed it myself,' she informed him proudly.

'I thought so the moment I saw it,' he answered, saying the wrong thing with cheerful ignorance.

'I'm afraid it is not as fashionable as I meant it to be!'

'I think it's a perfectly lovely hat,' he said loyally.

Again constraint settled down upon them. Frank Oliver broke the silence bravely.

'Little Lady, I didn't mean to tell you yet, but I can't help it. I love you. I want you. I loved you from the first moment I saw you standing there in your little black suit. Dearest, if two lonely people were together – why – there would be no more loneliness. And I'd work, oh! how I'd work! I'd paint you. I could, I know I could. Oh! my little girl, I can't live without you. I can't indeed –'

His little lady was looking at him very steadily. But what she said was quite the last thing he expected her to say. Very quietly and distinctly she said: 'You *bought* that handkerchief!'

He was amazed at this proof of feminine perspicacity, and still more amazed at her remembering it against him now. Surely, after this lapse of time, it might have been forgiven him.

'Yes, I did,' he acknowledged humbly. 'I wanted an excuse to speak to you. Are you very angry?' He waited meekly for her words of condemnation.

'I think it was sweet of you!' cried the little lady with vehemence. 'Just sweet of you!' Her voice ended uncertainly.

Frank Oliver went on in his gruff tone:

'Tell me, child, is it impossible? I know I'm an ugly, rough old fellow . . .'

The Lonely Lady interrupted him.

'No, you're not! I wouldn't have you different, not in any way. I love you just as you are, do you understand? Not because I'm sorry for you, not because I'm alone in the world and want someone to be fond of me and take care of me – but because you're just – *you*. Now do you understand?'

'Is it true?' he asked half in a whisper.

And she answered steadily: 'Yes, it's true –' The wonder of it overpowered them.

At last he said whimsically: 'So we've fallen upon heaven, dearest!'

'In an ABC shop,' she answered in a voice that held tears and laughter.

But terrestrial heavens are short-lived. The little lady started up with an exclamation.

'I'd no idea how late it was! I must go at once.'

'I'll see you home.'

'No, no, *no!*'

He was forced to yield to her insistence, and merely accompanied her as far as the Tube station.

'Goodbye, dearest.' She clung to his hand with an intensity that he remembered afterwards.

'Only goodbye till tomorrow,' he answered cheerfully. 'Ten o'clock as usual, and we'll tell each other our names and our histories, and be frightfully practical and prosaic.'

'Goodbye to – heaven, though,' she whispered.

'It will be with us always, sweetheart!'

She smiled back at him, but with that same sad appeal that disquieted him and which he could not fathom. Then the relentless lift dragged her down out of sight.

IV

He was strangely disturbed by those last words of hers, but he put them resolutely out of his mind and substituted radiant anticipations of tomorrow in their stead.

At ten o'clock he was there, in the accustomed place. For the first time he noticed how malevolently the other idols looked down upon him. It almost seemed as if they were possessed of some secret evil knowledge affecting him, over which they were gloating. He was uneasily aware of their dislike.

The little lady was late. Why didn't she come? The atmosphere of this place was getting on his nerves. Never had his own little friend (*their* god) seemed so hopelessly impotent as today. A helpless lump of stone, hugging his own despair!

His cogitations were interrupted by a small, sharp-faced boy who had stepped up to him, and was earnestly scrutinizing him from head to foot. Apparently satisfied with the result of his observations, he held out a letter.

'For me?'

It had no superscription. He took it, and the sharp boy decamped with extraordinary rapidity.

Frank Oliver read the letter slowly and unbelievingly. It was quite short.

Dearest,

I can never marry you. Please forget that I ever came into your life at all, and try to forgive me if I have hurt you. Don't try to find me, because it will be no good. It is really 'goodbye'.

The Lonely Lady

There was a postscript which had evidently been scribbled at the last moment:

I do love you. I do indeed.

And that little impulsive postscript was all the comfort he had in the weeks that followed. Needless to say, he disobeyed her injunction 'not to try to find her', but all in vain. She had vanished completely, and he had no clue to trace her by. He advertised despairingly, imploring her in veiled terms at least to explain the mystery, but blank silence rewarded his efforts. She was gone, never to return.

And then it was that for the first time in his life he really began to paint. His technique had always been good. Now craftsmanship and inspiration went hand in hand.

The picture that made his name and brought him renown was accepted and hung in the Academy, and was accounted to be *the* picture of the year, no less for the exquisite treatment of the subject than for the masterly workmanship and technique. A certain amount of mystery, too, rendered it more interesting to the general outside public.

His inspiration had come quite by chance. A fairy story in a magazine had taken a hold on his imagination.

It was the story of a fortunate Princess who had always had everything she wanted. Did she express a wish? It was instantly gratified. A desire? It was granted. She had a devoted father and mother, great riches, beautiful clothes and jewels, slaves to wait upon her and fulfil her lightest whim, laughing maidens to bear her company, all that the heart of a Princess could desire. The handsomest and richest Princes paid her court and sued in vain for her hand, and were willing to kill any number of dragons to prove their devotion. And yet, the loneliness of the Princess was greater than that of the poorest beggar in the land.

He read no more. The ultimate fate of the Princess interested him not at all. A picture had risen up before him of the pleasure-laden Princess with the sad, solitary soul, surfeited with happiness, suffocated with luxury, starving in the Palace of Plenty.

He began painting with furious energy. The fierce joy of creation possessed him.

He represented the Princess surrounded by her court, reclining on a divan. A riot of Eastern colour pervaded the picture. The Princess wore a marvellous gown of strange-coloured embroideries; her golden hair fell round her, and on her head was a heavy jewelled circlet. Her maidens surrounded her, and Princes knelt at her feet bearing rich gifts. The whole scene was one of luxury and richness.

But the face of the Princess was turned away; she was oblivious of the laughter and mirth around her. Her gaze was fixed on a dark and shadowy corner where stood a seemingly incongruous object: a little grey stone idol with its head buried in its hand in a quaint abandonment of despair.

Was it so incongruous? The eyes of the young Princess rested on it with a strange sympathy, as though a dawning sense of her own isolation drew her glance irresistibly. They were akin, these two. The world was at her feet – yet she was alone: a Lonely Princess looking at a lonely little god.

All London talked of this picture, and Greta wrote a few hurried words of congratulation from Yorkshire, and Tom Hurley's wife besought Frank Oliver to 'come for a weekend and meet a really delightful girl, a great admirer of your work'. Frank Oliver laughed once sardonically, and threw the letter into the fire. Success had come – but what was the use of it? He only wanted one thing – that little lonely lady who had gone out of his life for ever.

V

It was Ascot Cup Day, and the policeman on duty in a certain section of the British Museum rubbed his eyes and wondered if he were dreaming, for one does not expect to see there an Ascot vision, in a lace frock and a marvellous hat, a veritable nymph as imagined by a Parisian genius. The policeman stared in rapturous admiration.

The lonely god was not perhaps so surprised. He

may have been in his way a powerful little god; at any rate, here was one worshipper brought back to the fold.

The Little Lonely Lady was staring up at him, and her lips moved in a rapid whisper.

'Dear little god, oh! dear little god, please help me! Oh, please do help me!'

Perhaps the little god was flattered. Perhaps, if he was indeed the ferocious, unappeasable deity Frank Oliver had imagined him, the long weary years and the march of civilization had softened his cold, stone heart. Perhaps the Lonely Lady had been right all along and he was really a kind little god. Perhaps it was merely a coincidence. However that may be, it was at that very moment that Frank Oliver walked slowly and sadly through the door of the Assyrian room.

He raised his head and saw the Parisian nymph.

In another moment his arm was round her, and she was stammering out rapid, broken words.

'I was so lonely – *you* know, you must have read that story I wrote; you couldn't have painted that picture unless you had, and unless you had understood. The Princess was I; I had everything, and yet I was lonely beyond words. One day I was going to a fortune-teller's, and I borrowed my maid's clothes. I came in here on the way and saw you looking at the little god. That's how it all began. I pretended – oh! it was hateful of me, and I went on pretending, and afterwards I didn't dare confess that I had told you such dreadful lies. I thought you would be disgusted at the way I had deceived you. I couldn't bear you to find out, so I went away. Then I wrote that story, and yesterday I saw your picture. It *was* your picture, wasn't it?'

Only the gods really know the word 'ingratitude'. It is to be presumed that the lonely little god knew the black ingratitude of human nature. As a divinity he had unique opportunities of observing it, yet in the hour of trial he who had had sacrifices innumerable offered to him, made sacrifice in his turn. He sacrificed his only two worshippers in a strange land, and it showed him to be a great little god in his way, since he sacrificed all that he had.

Through the chinks in his fingers he watched them go, hand in hand, without a backward glance, two happy people who had found heaven and had no need of him any longer.

What was he, after all, but a very lonely little god in a strange land?

Afterword

'The Lonely God' was first published in the *Royal Magazine* in July 1926. It is one of Christie's few purely romantic stories and she herself considered it to be 'regrettably sentimental'.

Nevertheless, the story is interesting for it foreshadows Christie's life-long interest in archaeology, which she identified as being her favourite study in her contribution to *Michael Parkinson's Confessions Album* (1973), a book published for charity. It was a common interest in archaeology that led to her meeting the man who became her second husband, the celebrated archaeologist Max Mallowan. For many years after the Second World War, she and Mallowan spent each spring at Nimrud in Assyria and Christie's own account of excavations at Tell Brak in Syria in 1937 and 1938, *Come, Tell Me How You Live* (1946), is an entertaining and informative guide to the sites and this important other side of her character. While she never, apparently, wrote while on expedition, her experiences did provide material for several novels, including the Poirot mysteries *Murder in Mesopotamia* (1936), *Death on the Nile* (1937) and *Appointment With Death* (1938), as well as the extraordinary *Death Comes as the End* (1944), which is set in ancient Egypt over two thousand years before the birth of Christ.

Manx Gold

Foreword

'Manx Gold' is no ordinary detective story; indeed, it is probably unique. The detectives are conventional enough but although they are confronted with a particularly brutal murder, the murderer's identity is not their main concern. They are rather more interested in unravelling a series of clues to the whereabouts of hidden treasure, a treasure whose existence was not confined to the printed page! Clearly, some explanation is required . . .

In the winter of 1929, Alderman Arthur B. Crookall had a novel idea. Crookall was the chairman of the 'June Effort', a committee responsible for boosting tourism to the Isle of Man, and his idea was that there should be a treasure hunt, inspired by the many legends of Manx smugglers and their long-forgotten hoards of booty. There would be real treasure, hidden about the island,

and clues to its location concealed in the framework of a detective story. Initially, some members of the committee expressed reservations about Crookall's proposal, but it was eventually endorsed. The committee agreed that the 'Isle of Man Treasure Hunt Scheme' should take place at the start of the holiday season and run at the same time as the International Tourist Trophy motorcycle races, then in their 24th year, and alongside other annual events such as the 'crowning of the Rose Queen' and the midnight yacht race.

But Crookall had to find someone to write the story around which the hunt would be based. Who better than Agatha Christie? Perhaps surprisingly, and for a fee of only £60, Christie accepted this, her most unusual commission. She visited the Isle of Man at the end of April 1930, staying as the guest of the Lieutenant Governor of the island before returning to Devon where her daughter was ill. Christie and Crookall spent several days discussing the treasure hunt, and visited various sites in order to decide where the treasure should be hidden and how the clues should be composed.

The resulting story, 'Manx Gold', was published in five instalments towards the end of May by the *Daily Dispatch*. The *Dispatch* was published in Manchester and had been selected by the committee presumably because it was felt to be the newspaper that potential

English visitors to the island were most likely to see. 'Manx Gold' was also reprinted in booklet form, and a quarter of a million copies were distributed to guest-houses and hotels across the island. The five clues were published separately (their location in the text is marked by †) and as the date on which the first was due to appear in the *Dispatch* drew nearer, the 'June Effort' Committee appealed to everyone to 'co-operate in order to obtain as much publicity as possible' for the hunt. More tourists meant more tourist revenue, and the hunt was also drawn to the attention of several hundred 'Homecomers', who had emigrated from the island to the United States and were due to return as honoured guests in June. In the words of the publicity at the time, it was 'an opportunity for all Amateur Detectives to test their skill'! To compete with Juan and Fenella, you were advised – like them – to equip yourself with 'several excellent maps . . . various guide books descriptive of the Island . . . a book on folklore [and] a book on the history of the Island'. The solutions to the clues are given at the end of the story.

Manx Gold

I

Old Mylecharane liv'd up on the broo.
Where Jurby slopes down to the wold,
His croft was all golden with cushag and furze,
His daughter was fair to behold.

'O father, they say you've plenty of store,
But hidden all out of the way.
No gold can I see, but its glint on the gorse;
Then what have you done with it, pray?'

'My gold is locked up in a coffer of oak,
Which I dropped in the tide and it sank,
And there it lies fixed like an anchor of hope,
All bright and as safe as the bank.'

'I like that song,' I said appreciatively, as Fenella finished.

'You should do,' said Fenella. 'It's about our ancestor,

yours and mine. Uncle Myles's grandfather. He made a fortune out of smuggling and hid it somewhere, and no one ever knew where.'

Ancestry is Fenella's strong point. She takes an interest in all her forebears. My tendencies are strictly modern. The difficult present and the uncertain future absorb all my energy. But I like hearing Fenella singing old Manx ballads.

Fenella is very charming. She is my first cousin and also, from time to time, my fiancée. In moods of financial optimism we are engaged. When a corresponding wave of pessimism sweeps over us and we realize that we shall not be able to marry for at least ten years, we break it off.

'Didn't anyone ever try to find the treasure?' I inquired.

'Of course. But they never did.'

'Perhaps they didn't look scientifically.'

'Uncle Myles had a jolly good try,' said Fenella. 'He said anyone with intelligence ought to be able to solve a little problem like that.'

That sounded to me very like our Uncle Myles, a cranky and eccentric old gentleman, who lived in the Isle of Man, and who was much given to didactic pronouncements.

It was at that moment that the post came – and the letter!

142

'Good Heavens,' cried Fenella. 'Talk of the devil – I mean angels – Uncle Myles is dead!'

Both she and I had only seen our eccentric relative on two occasions, so we could neither of us pretend to a very deep grief. The letter was from a firm of lawyers in Douglas, and it informed us that under the will of Mr Myles Mylecharane, deceased, Fenella and I were joint inheritors of his estate, which consisted of a house near Douglas, and an infinitesimal income. Enclosed was a sealed envelope, which Mr Mylecharane had directed should be forwarded to Fenella at his death. This letter we opened and read its surprising contents. I reproduce it in full, since it was a truly characteristic document.

'*My dear Fenella and Juan (for I take it that where one of you is the other will not be far away! Or so gossip has whispered), You may remember having heard me say that anyone displaying a little intelligence could easily find the treasure concealed by my amiable scoundrel of a grandfather. I displayed that intelligence – and my reward was four chests of solid gold – quite like a fairy story, is it not?*

Of living relations I have only four, you two, my nephew Ewan Corjeag, whom I have always heard is a thoroughly bad lot, and a cousin, a Doctor Fayll, of whom I have heard very little, and that little not always good.

My estate proper I am leaving to you and Fenella, but

143

I feel a certain obligation laid upon me with regard to this 'treasure' which has fallen to my lot solely through my own ingenuity. My amiable ancestor would not, I feel, be satisfied for me to pass it on tamely by inheritance. So I, in my turn, have devised a little problem.

There are still four 'chests' of treasure (though in a more modern form than gold ingots or coins) and there are to be four competitors – my four living relations. It would be fairest to assign one 'chest' to each – but the world, my children, is not fair. The race is to the swiftest – and often to the most unscrupulous!

Who am I to go against Nature? You must pit your wits against the other two. There will be, I fear, very little chance for you. Goodness and innocence are seldom rewarded in this world. So strongly do I feel this that I have deliberately cheated (unfairness again, you notice!). This letter goes to you twenty-four hours in advance of the letters to the other two. Thus you will have a very good chance of securing the first "treasure" – twenty-four hours' start, if you have any brains at all, ought to be sufficient.

The clues for finding this treasure are to be found at my house in Douglas. The clues for the second "treasure" will not be released till the first treasure is found. In the second and succeeding cases, therefore, you will all start even. You have my good wishes for success, and nothing would please me better than for you to acquire all four "chests", but for the reasons which I have already stated I

think that most unlikely. Remember that no scruples will
stand in dear Ewan's way. Do not make the mistake of
trusting him in any respect. As to Dr Richard Fayll, I
know little about him, but he is, I fancy, a dark horse.

Good luck to you both, but with little hopes of your
success,

Your affectionate Uncle,
Myles Mylecharane'

As we reached the signature, Fenella made a leap from
my side.

'What is it?' I cried.

Fenella was rapidly turning the pages of an ABC.

'We must get to the Isle of Man as soon as possible,'
she cried. 'How dare he say we were good and innocent
and stupid? I'll show him! Juan, we're going to find all
four of these "chests" and get married and live happily
ever afterwards, with Rolls-Royces and footmen and
marble baths. But we *must* get to the Isle of Man
at once.'

II

It was twenty-four hours later. We had arrived in
Douglas, interviewed the lawyers, and were now
at Maughold House facing Mrs Skillicorn, our late

Uncle's housekeeper, a somewhat formidable woman who nevertheless relented a little before Fenella's eagerness.

'Queer ways he had,' she said. 'Liked to set everyone puzzling and contriving.'

'But the clues,' cried Fenella. 'The clues?'

Deliberately, as she did everything, Mrs Skillicorn left the room. She returned after an absence of some minutes and held out a folded piece of paper.

We unfolded it eagerly. It contained a doggerel rhyme in my Uncle's crabbed handwriting.†

> *Four points of the compass so there be*
> *S., and W., N. and E.*
> *East winds are bad for man and beast.*
> *Go south and west and*
> *North not east.*

'Oh!' said Fenella, blankly.

'Oh!' said I, with much the same intonation.

Mrs Skillicorn smiled on us with gloomy relish.

'Not much sense to it, is there?' she said helpfully.

'It – I don't see how to begin,' said Fenella, piteously.

'Beginning,' I said, with a cheerfulness I did not feel, 'is always the difficulty. Once we get going –'

Mrs Skillicorn smiled more grimly than ever. She was a depressing woman.

'Can't you help us?' asked Fenella, coaxingly.

'I know nothing about the silly business. Didn't confide in me, your uncle didn't. I have told him to put his money in the bank, and no nonsense. I never knew what he was up to.'

'He never went out with any chests – or anything of that kind?'

'That he didn't.'

'You don't know when he hid the stuff – whether it was lately or long ago?'

Mrs Skillicorn shook her head.

'Well,' I said, trying to rally. 'There are two possibilities. Either the treasure is hidden here, in the actual grounds, or else it may be hidden anywhere on the Island. It depends on the bulk, of course.'

A sudden brain-wave occurred to Fenella.

'You haven't noticed anything missing?' she said. 'Among my Uncle's things, I mean?'

'Why, now, it's odd your saying that –'

'You have, then?'

'As I say, it's odd your saying that. Snuffboxes – there's at least four of them I can't lay my hand on anywhere.'

'Four of them!' cried Fenella, 'that must be it! We're on the track. Let's go out in the garden and look about.'

'There's nothing there,' said Mrs Skillicorn. 'I'd

147

know if there were. Your Uncle couldn't have buried anything in the garden without my knowing about it.'

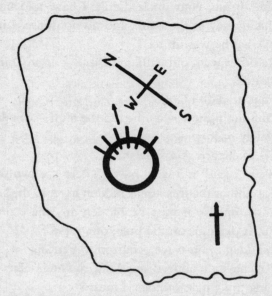

'Points of the compass are mentioned,' I said. 'The first thing we need is a map of the Island.'

'There's one of that desk,' said Mrs Skillicorn.

Fenella unfolded it eagerly. Something fluttered out as she did so. I caught it.

'Hullo,' I said. 'This looks like a further clue.'

We both went over it eagerly.

It appeared to be a rude kind of map. There was a cross on it and a circle and a pointing arrow, and directions were roughly indicated, but it was hardly illuminating. We studied it in silence.†

'It's not very illuminating, is it?' said Fenella.

'Naturally it wants puzzling over,' I said. 'We can't expect it to leap to the eye.'

Mrs Skillicorn interrupted with a suggestion of supper, to which we agreed thankfully.

'And could we have some coffee?' said Fenella. 'Lots of it – very black.'

Mrs Skillicorn provided us with an excellent meal, and at its conclusion a large jug of coffee made its appearance.

'And now,' said Fenella, 'we must get down to it.'

'The first thing,' I said, 'is direction. This seems to point clearly to the north-east of the Island.'

'It seems so. Let's look at the map.'

We studied the map attentively.

'It all depends on how you take the thing,' said Fenella. 'Does the cross represent the treasure? Or is it something like a church? There really ought to be rules!'

'That would make it too easy.'

'I suppose it would. Why are there little lines one side of the circle and not the other.'

'I don't know.'

'Are there any more maps anywhere?'

We were sitting in the library. There were several excellent maps. There were also various guide books descriptive of the Island. There was a book on folklore. There was a book on the history of the Island. We read them all.

And at last we formed a possible theory.

'It does seem to fit,' said Fenella at last. 'I mean the two together is a likely conjunction which doesn't seem to occur anywhere else.'

'It's worth trying, anyhow,' I said. 'I don't think we can do anything more tonight. Tomorrow, first thing, we'll hire a car and go off and try our luck.'

'It's tomorrow now,' said Fenella. 'Half-past two! Just fancy!'

III

Early morning saw us on the road. We had hired a car for a week, arranging to drive it ourselves. Fenella's spirits rose as we sped along the excellent road, mile after mile.

'If only it wasn't for the other two, what fun this would be,' she said. 'This is where the Derby was originally run, wasn't it? Before it was changed to Epsom. How queer that is to think of!'

I drew her attention to a farmhouse.

150

'That must be where there is said to be a secret passage running under the sea to that island.'

'What fun! I love secret passages, don't you? Oh! Juan, we're getting quite near now. I'm terribly excited. If we should be right!'

Five minutes later we abandoned the car.

'Everything's in the right position,' said Fenella, tremulously.

We walked on.

'Six of them – that's right. Now between these two. Have you got the compass?'

Five minutes later, we were standing facing each other, an incredulous joy on our faces – and on my outstretched palm lay an antique snuffbox.

We had been successful!

On our return to Maughold House, Mrs Skillicorn met us with the information that two gentlemen had arrived. One had departed again, but the other was in the library.

A tall, fair man, with a florid face, rose smilingly from an armchair as we entered the room.

'Mr Faraker and Miss Mylecharane? Delighted to meet you. I am your distant cousin, Dr Fayll. Amusing game all this, isn't it?'

His manner was urbane and pleasant, but I took an immediate dislike to him. I felt that in some way the man was dangerous. His pleasant manner was, somehow, *too* pleasant, and his eyes never met yours fairly.

'I'm afraid we've got bad news for you,' I said. 'Miss Mylecharane and myself have already discovered the first "treasure".'

He took it very well.

'Too bad – too bad. Posts from here must be odd. Barford and I started at once.'

We did not dare to confess the perfidy of Uncle Myles.

'Anyway, we shall all start fair for the second round,' said Fenella.

'Splendid. What about getting down to the clues right away? Your excellent Mrs – er – Skillicorn holds them, I believe?'

'That wouldn't be fair to Mr Corjeag,' said Fenella, quickly. 'We must wait for him.'

'True, true – I had forgotten. We must get in touch with him as quickly as possible. I will see to that – you two must be tired out and want to rest.'

Thereupon he took his departure. Ewan Corjeag must have been unexpectedly difficult to find, for it was not till nearly eleven o'clock that night that Dr Fayll rang up. He suggested that he and Ewan should come over to Maughold House at ten o'clock the following morning, when Mrs Skillicorn could hand us out the clues.

'That will do splendidly,' said Fenella. 'Ten o'clock tomorrow.'

We retired to bed tired but happy.

IV

The following morning we were aroused by Mrs Skillicorn, completely shaken out of her usual pessimistic calm.

'Whatever do you think?' she panted. 'The house has been broken into.'

'Burglars?' I exclaimed, incredulously. 'Has anything been taken?'

'Not a thing – and that's the odd part of it! No doubt they were after the silver – but the door being locked on the outside they couldn't get any further.'

Fenella and I accompanied her to the scene of the outrage, which happened to be in her own sitting-room. The window there had undeniably been forced, yet nothing seemed to have been taken. It was all rather curious.

'I don't see what they can have been looking for?' said Fenella.

'It's not as though there were a "treasure chest" hidden in the house,' I agreed facetiously. Suddenly an idea flashed into my mind. I turned to Mrs Skillicorn.

'The clues – the clues you were to give us this morning?'

'Why to be sure – they're in that top drawer.' She went across to it. 'Why – I do declare – there's nothing here! They're gone!'

'Not burglars,' I said. 'Our esteemed relations!' And I remember Uncle Myles's warning on the subject of unscrupulous dealing. Clearly he had known what he was talking about. A dirty trick!

'Hush,' said Fenella, suddenly, holding up a finger. 'What was that?'

The sound she had caught came plainly to our ears. It was a groan and it came from outside. We went to the window and leaned out. There was a shrubbery growing against this side of the house and we could see nothing; but the groan came again, and we could see that the bushes seemed to have been disturbed and trampled.

We hurried down and out round the house. The first thing we found was a fallen ladder, showing how the thieves had reached the window. A few steps further brought us to where a man was lying.

He was a youngish man, dark, and he was evidently badly injured, for his head was lying in a pool of blood. I knelt down beside him.

'We must get a doctor at once. I'm afraid he's dying.'

The gardener was sent off hurriedly. I slipped my hand into his breast pocket and brought out a pocket book. On it were the initials EC.

'Ewan Corjeag,' said Fenella.

The man's eyes opened. He said, faintly: 'Fell from ladder . . .' then lost consciousness again.

Close by his head was a large jagged stone stained with blood.

'It's clear enough,' I said. 'The ladder slipped and he fell, striking his head on this stone. I'm afraid it's done for him, poor fellow.'

'So you think that was it?' said Fenella, in an odd tone of voice.

But at that moment the doctor arrived. He held out little hope of recovery. Ewan Corjeag was moved into the house and a nurse was sent for to take charge of him. Nothing could be done, and he would die a couple of hours later.

We had been sent for and were standing by his bed. His eyes opened and flickered.

'We are your cousins Juan and Fenella,' I said. 'Is there anything we can do?'

He made a faint negative motion of the head. A whisper came from his lips. I bent to catch it.

'Do you want the clue? I'm done. Don't let Fayll do you down.'

'Yes,' said Fenella. 'Tell me.'

Something like a grin came over his face.

'*D'ye ken* –' he began.

Then suddenly his head fell over sideways and he died.

V

'I don't like it,' said Fenella, suddenly.

'What don't you like?'

'Listen, Juan. Ewan stole those clues – he admits falling from the ladder. *Then where are they?* We've seen all the contents of his pockets. There were three sealed envelopes, so Mrs Skillicorn says. Those sealed envelopes aren't there.'

'What do you think, then?'

'I think there was someone else there, someone who jerked away the ladder so that he fell. And that stone – he never fell on it – it was brought from some distance away – I've found the mark. He was deliberately bashed on the head with it.'

'But Fenella – that's murder!'

'Yes,' said Fenella, very white. 'It's murder. Remember, Dr Fayll never turned up at ten o'clock this morning. Where is he?'

'You think he's the murderer?'

'Yes. You know – this treasure – it's a lot of money, Juan.'

'And we've no idea where to look for him,' I said. 'A

pity Corjeag couldn't have finished what he was going to say.'

'There's one thing might help. This was in his hand.'
She handed me a torn snap-shot.†

'Suppose it's a clue. The murderer snatched it away and never noticed he'd left a corner of it behind. If we were to find the other half –'

'To do that,' I said, 'we must find the second treasure. Let's look at this thing.'

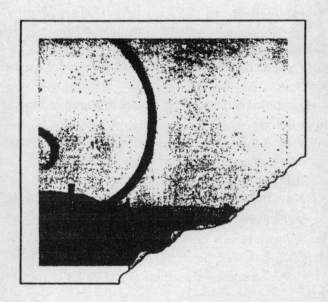

'H'm,' I said, 'there's nothing much to go by. That seems a kind of tower in the middle of the circle, but it would be very hard to identify.'

Fenella nodded.

'Dr Fayll has the important half. He knows where to look. We've got to find that man, Juan, and watch him. Of course, we won't let him see we suspect.'

'I wonder whereabouts in the Island he is this minute. If we only knew —'

My mind went back to the dying man. Suddenly, I sat up excitedly.

'Fenella,' I said, 'Corjeag wasn't Scotch?'

'No, of course not.'

'Well, then, don't you see? What he meant, I mean?'

'No?'

I scribbled something on a piece of paper and tossed it to her.

'What's this?'

'The name of a firm that might help us.'

'Bellman and True. Who are they? Lawyers?'

'No – they're more in our line – private detectives.'

And I proceeded to explain.

VI

'Dr Fayll to see you,' said Mrs Skillicorn.

We looked at each other. Twenty-four hours had elapsed. We had returned from our quest successful for the second time. Not wishing to draw attention to ourselves, we had journeyed in the Snaefell – a charabanc.

'I wonder if he knows we saw him in the distance?' murmured Fenella.

'It's extraordinary. If it hadn't been for the hint that photograph gave us –'

'Hush – and do be careful, Juan. He must be simply furious at our having outwitted him, in spite of everything.'

No trace of it appeared in the doctor's manner, however. He entered the room his urbane and charming self, and I felt my faith in Fenella's theory dwindling.

'What a shocking tragedy!' he said. 'Poor Corjeag. I suppose he was – well – trying to steal a march on us. Retribution was swift. Well, well – we scarcely knew him, poor fellow. You must have wondered why I didn't turn up this morning as arranged. I got a fake message – Corjeag's doing, I suppose – it sent me off on a wild-goose chase right across the Island. And now you two have romped home again. How do you do it?'

There was a note of really eager inquiry in his voice which did not escape me.

'Cousin Ewan was fortunately able to speak just before he died,' said Fenella.

I was watching the man, and I could swear I saw alarm leap into his eyes at her words.

'Eh – eh? What's that?' he said.

'He was just able to give us a clue as to the whereabouts of the treasure,' explained Fenella.

'Oh! I see – I see. I've been clean out of things – though, curiously enough, I myself was in that part of the Island. You may have seen me strolling round.'

'We were so busy,' said Fenella, apologetically.

'Of course, of course. You must have run across the thing more or less by accident. Lucky young people, aren't you? Well, what's the next programme? Will Mrs Skillicorn oblige us with the new clues?'

But it seemed that this third set of clues had been deposited with the lawyers, and we all three repaired to the lawyer's office, where the sealed envelopes were handed over to us.

The contents were simple. A map with a certain area marked off on it, and a paper of directions attached.†

In '85, this place made history.
Ten paces from the landmark to
The east, then an equal ten
Paces north. Stand there
Looking east. Two trees are in the
Line of vision. One of them
Was sacred in this island. Draw
A circle five feet from
The Spanish chestnut and,
With head bent, walk round. Look well. You'll find.

'Looks as though we were going to tread on each other's toes a bit today,' commented the doctor.

True to my policy of apparent friendliness, I offered him a lift in our car, which he accepted. We had lunch at Port Erin, and then started on our search.

I had debated in my own mind the reason of my uncle's depositing this particular set of clues with his lawyer. Had he foreseen the possibility of a theft? And had he determined that not more than one set of clues should fall into the thief's possession?

The treasure hunt this afternoon was not without its humour. The area of search was limited, and we were continually in sight of each other. We eyed each other suspiciously, each trying to determine whether the other was farther on or had had a brain-wave.

'This is all part of Uncle Myles's plan,' said Fenella. 'He wanted us to watch each other and go through all the agonies of thinking the other person was getting there.'

'Come,' I said. 'Let's get down to it scientifically. We've got one definite clue to start on. "*In '85 this place made history.*" Look up the reference books we've got with us and see if we can't hunt that down. Once we get that –'

'He's looking in that hedge,' interrupted Fenella. 'Oh! I can't bear it. If he's got it –'

'Attend to me,' I said firmly. 'There's really only one way to go about it – the proper way.'

'There are so few trees on the Island that it would be much simpler just to look for a chestnut tree!' said Fenella.

I pass over the next hour. We grew hot and despondent – and all the time we were tortured with fear that Fayll might be succeeding whilst we failed.

'I remember once reading in a detective story,' I said, 'how a fellow stuck a paper of writing in a bath of acid – and all sorts of other words came out.'

'Do you think – but we haven't got a bath of acid!'

'I don't think Uncle Myles could expect expert chemical knowledge. But there's common-or-garden heat –'

We slipped round the corner of a hedge and in a minute or two I had kindled a few twigs. I held the paper as close to the blaze as I dared. Almost at once I was rewarded by seeing characters begin to appear at the foot of the sheet. There were just two words.

'Kirkhill Station,' read out Fenella.

Just at that moment Fayll came round the corner. Whether he had heard or not we had no means of judging. He showed nothing.

'But, Juan,' said Fenella, when he moved away,

'there isn't a Kirkhill Station!' She held out the map as she spoke.

'No,' I said, examining it, 'but look here.'

And with a pencil I drew a line on it.

'Of course! And somewhere on that line –'

'Exactly.'

'But I wish we knew the exact spot.'

It was then that my second brain-wave came to me.

'We do!' I cried, and, seizing the pencil again, I said: 'Look!'

Fenella uttered a cry.

'How idiotic!' she cried. 'And how marvellous! What a sell! Really, Uncle Myles was a most ingenious old gentleman!'

VII

The time had come for the last clue. This, the lawyer had informed us, was not in his keeping. It was to be posted to us on receipt of a postcard sent by him. He would impart no further information.

Nothing arrived, however, on the morning it should have done, and Fenella and I went through agonies, believing that Fayll had managed somehow to intercept our letter. The next day, however, our fears were calmed and the mystery explained when we received the following illiterate scrawl:

> 'Dear Sir or Madam,
>
> Escuse delay but have been all sixes and sevens but i do now as mr Mylecharane axed me to and send you the piece of riting wot as been in my family many long years the wot he wanted it for i do not know. thanking you i am
>
> Mary Kerruish'

'Post mark – Bride,' I remarked. 'Now for the "piece of riting handed down in my family"!'†

> Upon a rock, a sign you'll see.
> O, Tell me what the point of
> That may be? Well, firstly, (A). Near
> By you'll find, quite suddenly, the light
> You seek. Then (B). A house. A
> Cottage with a thatch and wall.
> A meandering lane near by. That's all.

'It's very unfair to begin with a rock,' said Fenella. 'There are rocks everywhere. How can you tell which one has the sign on it?'

'If we could settle on the district,' I said, 'it ought to be fairly easy to find the rock. It must have a mark on it pointing in a certain direction, and in that direction

165

there will be something hidden which will throw light on the finding of the treasure.'

'I think you're right,' said Fenella.

'That's A. The new clue will give us a hint where B, the cottage, is to be found. The treasure itself is hidden down a lane alongside the cottage. But clearly we've got to find A first.'

Owing to the difficulty of the initial step, Uncle Myles's last problem proved a real teaser. To Fenella falls the distinction of unravelling it – and even then she did not accomplish it for nearly a week. Now and then we had come across Fayll in our search of rocky districts, but the area was a wide one.

When we finally made our discovery it was late in the evening. Too late, I said, to start off to the place indicated. Fenella disagreed.

'Supposing Fayll finds it, too,' she said. 'And we wait till tomorrow and he starts off tonight. How we should kick ourselves!'

Suddenly, a marvellous idea occurred to me.

'Fenella,' I said, 'do you still believe that Fayll murdered Ewan Corjeag?'

'I do.'

'Then I think that now we've got our chance to bring the crime home to him.'

'That man makes me shiver. He's bad all through. Tell me.'

'Advertise the fact that we've found A. Then start off. Ten to one he'll follow us. It's a lonely place – just what would suit his book. He'll come out in the open if we pretend to find the treasure.'

'And then?'

'And then,' I said, 'he'll have a little surprise.'

VIII

It was close on midnight. We had left the car some distance away and were creeping along by the side of a wall. Fenella had a powerful flashlight which she was using. I myself carried a revolver. I was taking no chances.

Suddenly, with a low cry, Fenella stopped.

'Look, Juan,' she cried. 'We've got it. At last.'

For a moment I was off my guard. Led by instinct I whirled round – but too late. Fayll stood six paces away and his revolver covered us both.

'Good evening,' he said. 'This trick is mine. You'll hand over that treasure, if you please.'

'Would you like me also to hand over something else?' I asked. 'Half a snap-shot torn from a dying man's hand? *You have the other half, I think.*'

His hand wavered.

'What are you talking about?' he growled.

'The truth's known,' I said. 'You and Corjeag were there together. You pulled away the ladder and crashed his head with that stone. The police are cleverer than you imagine, Dr Fayll.'

'They know, do they? Then, by Heaven, I'll swing for three murders instead of one!'

'Drop, Fenella,' I screamed. And at the same minute his revolver barked loudly.

We had both dropped in the heather, and before he could fire again uniformed men sprang out from behind the wall where they had been hiding. A moment later Fayll had been handcuffed and led away.

I caught Fenella in my arms.

'I knew I was right,' she said tremulously.

'Darling!' I cried, 'it was too risky. He might have shot you.'

'But he didn't,' said Fenella. 'And we know where the treasure is.'

'Do we?'

'I do. See –' she scribbled a word. 'We'll look for it tomorrow. There can't be many hiding places there, I should say.'

IX

It was just noon when:

'Eureka!' said Fenella, softly. 'The fourth snuffbox. We've got them all. Uncle Myles would be pleased. And now –'

'Now,' I said, 'we can be married and live together happily ever afterwards.'

'We'll live in the Isle of Man,' said Fenella.

'On Manx Gold,' I said, and laughed aloud for sheer happiness.

Afterword

Juan and Fenella are first cousins and very much in the mould of Tommy and Tuppence Beresford, the eponymous detectives in *Partners in Crime* (1929) and several later novels. They are also closely related to the young 'sleuths' of any of Christie's early thrillers such as *The Secret of Chimneys* (1925) and *Why Didn't They Ask Evans?* (1934). In reality, as in the story, the 'treasure' took the form of four snuffboxes, each about the size of a matchbox. The snuffboxes each contained an eighteenth-century Manx halfpenny, which had a hole in it, through which was tied a length of coloured ribbon. Each snuffbox also contained a neatly folded document, executed with many flourishes in Indian ink and signed by Alderman Crookall, which directed the finder to report at once to the Clerk at the Town Hall in Douglas, the capital of the Isle of Man. Finders were instructed to take with them the snuffbox and its contents in order to claim a prize of £100 (equivalent to around £3,000 today). They also had to bring with them proof of identity for only visitors to the island were allowed to search for the treasure; Manx residents were debarred.

'A little intelligence could easily find the treasure'

The sole purpose of the first clue in 'Manx Gold', the rhyme which began 'Four points of the compass so there be' and published in the *Daily Dispatch* on Saturday 31 May, was to indicate that the four treasures would be found in the north, south and west of the island but not in the east. The clue to the location of the first snuffbox was in fact the second clue, a map published on 7 June. However, the treasure had already been found by this time because sufficient clues to its location were contained in the story. The finder was a tailor from Inverness, William Shaw, who was reported in local newspapers to have celebrated the find by running in a circle, waving the snuffbox in the air, 'while his good lady was too excited to speak for several minutes'!

The most important clue was Fenella's remark that the hiding place was near the place 'where the Derby was originally run . . . before it was changed to Epsom'. This is a reference to the famous English horse-race, which was first run at Derbyhaven in the south-east of the Isle of Man. The 'quite near' island to which 'a secret passage' was rumoured to run from a farmhouse can easily be identified as St Michael's Isle on which, in addition to the twelfth-century chapel of St Michael, is a circular stone tower known as the Derby Fort, from which the island gets its alternative name, Fort Island – 'the two together is a likely conjunction which doesn't seem to occur anywhere else'. The fort was represented in the map by a circle with six lines projecting from it to represent the six historic cannons – 'six of them' – in the fort; the chapel was represented by a cross.

The small pewter snuffbox was hidden on a rocky ledge running in a north-easterly direction from between the middle two cannon – 'between these two – have you got the compass?' – while Juan's initial suggestion that the clue 'points to the north-east of the island' was a red herring.

'Too easy'

The second snuffbox, apparently constructed from horn, was located on 9 June by Richard Highton, a Lancashire builder. As Fenella made clear to the murderous Dr Fayll, Ewan Corjeag's dying words 'D'ye ken –' are a clue to the whereabouts of the treasure. In fact, they are the opening words of the traditional English song *John Peel* about a Cumbrian huntsman and, when Juan suggested that 'Bellman and True' was 'the name of a firm that might help us', he was not referring to the 'firm of lawyers in Douglas' mentioned at the beginning of the story but to two of John Peel's hounds, as named in the song. With these clues, the subject of the 'torn snap-shot', which was published as the third clue on 9 June, would not have been 'very hard to identify'; they were the ruins of the fourteenth-century Peel Castle on St Patrick's Isle, and curved lines along the photograph's left-hand edge were the curlicues on the arm of a bench on Peel Hill, which looks down on the castle and under which the snuffbox was hidden. The charabanc journey to Snaefell, the highest peak on the Isle of Man, was a red herring.

'More or less by accident'

The third 'treasure' was found by Mr Herbert Elliott, a Manx-born ship's engineer living in Liverpool. Mr Elliott later claimed that he had not read 'Manx Gold' nor even studied the clues, but had simply decided on a likely area where, very early on the morning of 8 July, he chanced upon the snuffbox, hidden in a gully.

The principal clue to its whereabouts was hidden in the fourth clue, published on 14 June (the verse beginning 'In '85, this place made history'), in which the second word of each line spells out the message:

'85 paces east north east of sacred circle Spanish Head.'

The 'sacred circle' is the Meayll circle on Mull Hill, a megalithic monument a little over a mile from Spanish Head, the most southerly point of the island. The references to an important event 'in '85' and a Spanish chestnut, which from contemporary accounts proved a diversion for many searchers, were false leads. As for 'Kirkhill Station', the clue uncovered by Juan, Fenella rightly said that there was no such place. However, there is a village called Kirkhill, and there is also a railway station at Port Erin, where Juan and Fenella had had lunch before starting their search. If a line is drawn from Kirkhill to Port Erin and continued southwards, it eventually crosses the Meayll circle, 'the exact spot' identified by Juan.

'A real teaser'

Unfortunately, as was the case with the clues to the location of the third snuffbox, those for the fourth were never solved. The fifth and final clue, the verse beginning 'Upon a rock, a sign you'll see' was published on 21 June, but on 10 July, at the end of the extended period allowed for the hunt, which had originally been intended to finish at the end of June, the final treasure was 'lifted' by the Mayor of Douglas. Two days later, as a 'sequel' to the story, the *Daily Dispatch* published a photograph of the event and Christie's explanation of the final clue:

That last clue still makes me smile when I remember the time we wasted looking for rocks with a sign on them. The real clue was so simple – the words 'sixes and sevens' in the covering letter.

Take the sixth and seventh word of each line of the verse, and you get this, '*You'll see. Point of (A). Near the light house a wall.*' Seek the point of (A) we identified as the Point of Ayre. We spent some time finding the right wall, and the treasure itself was not there. Instead, there were four figures – 2, 5, 6 and 9 scrawled on a stone.

Apply them to the letters of the first line of the verse, and you get the word '*park*'. There is only one real park in the Isle of Man, at Ramsey. We searched that park, and found at last what we sought.

The thatched building in question was a small refreshment kiosk, and the path leading past it ran up to an ivy-covered wall which was the hiding-place of the elusive snuffbox. The fact that the letter had been posted in Bride was an additional clue as this village is near the lighthouse at the Point of Ayre, the northernmost tip of the island.

It is impossible to judge whether or not 'Manx Gold' was a successful means of promoting tourism to the Isle of Man. Certainly, it appears that there were more visitors in 1930 than in previous years, but how far that increase could be ascribed to the treasure hunt is far from clear. Contemporary press reports show that there were many who doubted that it had been of any real value and, at a civic lunch to mark the end of the hunt, Alderman Crookall responded to a vote of thanks by railing against those who had failed to talk up the hunt – they were 'slackers and grousers who never did anything but offer criticism'.

The fact that islanders were not allowed to take part in the hunt may have been a cause of apathy among the islanders, even though the *Daily Dispatch* offered the Manx resident with whom each finder was staying a prize of five guineas, equivalent to about £150 today. This may also have accounted for various acts of gentle 'sabotage' such as the laying of false snuffboxes and spoof clues, including a rock on which the word 'Lift' was painted but under which was nothing more interesting than discarded peel.

While there has never been any other event similar to the Isle of Man treasure hunt, Agatha Christie *did* go on

Agatha Christie

to write mysteries with a similar theme. Most obvious of these is the challenge laid down to Charmian Stroud and Edward Rossiter by their eccentric Uncle Mathew in 'Strange Jest', a Miss Marple story first published in 1941 as 'A Case of Buried Treasure' and collected in *Miss Marple's Final Cases* (1979). There is also a similarly structured 'murder hunt' in the Poirot novel, *Dead Man's Folly* (1956).

Within a Wall

I

It was Mrs Lemprière who discovered the existence of Jane Haworth. It would be, of course. Somebody once said that Mrs Lemprière was easily the most hated woman in London, but that, I think, is an exaggeration. She has certainly a knack of tumbling on the one thing you wish to keep quiet about, and she does it with real genius. It is always an accident.

In this case we had been having tea in Alan Everard's studio. He gave these teas occasionally, and used to stand about in corners, wearing very old clothes, rattling the coppers in his trouser pockets and looking profoundly miserable.

I do not suppose anyone will dispute Everard's claim to genius at this date. His two most famous pictures, *Colour*, and *The Connoisseur*, which belong to his early period, before he became a fashionable portrait painter, were purchased by the nation last year, and for once the choice

179

went unchallenged. But at the date of which I speak, Everard was only beginning to come into his own, and we were free to consider that we had discovered him.

It was his wife who organized these parties. Everard's attitude to her was a peculiar one. That he adored her was evident, and only to be expected. Adoration was Isobel's due. But he seemed always to feel himself slightly in her debt. He assented to anything she wished, not so much through tenderness as through an unalterable conviction that she had a right to her own way. I suppose that was natural enough, too, when one comes to think of it.

For Isobel Loring had been really very celebrated. When she came out she had been *the* débutante of the season. She had everything except money; beauty, position, breeding, brains. Nobody expected her to marry for love. She wasn't that kind of girl. In her second season she had three strings to her bow, the heir to a dukedom, a rising politician, and a South African millionaire. And then, to everyone's surprise, she married Alan Everard – a struggling young painter whom no one had ever heard of.

It is a tribute to her personality, I think, that everyone went on calling her Isobel Loring. Nobody ever alluded to her as Isobel Everard. It would be: 'I saw Isobel Loring this morning. Yes – with her husband, young Everard, the painter fellow.'

180

People said Isobel had 'done for herself'. It would, I think, have 'done' for most men to be known as 'Isobel Loring's husband'. But Everard was different. Isobel's talent for success hadn't failed her after all. Alan Everard painted *Colour*.

I suppose everyone knows the picture: a stretch of road with a trench dug down it, the turned earth, reddish in colour, a shining length of brown glazed drainpipe and the huge navvy, resting for a minute on his spade – a Herculean figure in stained corduroys with a scarlet neckerchief. His eyes look out at you from the canvas, without intelligence, without hope, but with a dumb unconscious pleading, the eyes of a magnificent brute beast. It is a flaming thing – a symphony of orange and red. A lot has been written about its symbolism, about what it is meant to express. Alan Everard himself says he didn't mean it to express anything. He was, he said, nauseated by having had to look at a lot of pictures of Venetian sunsets, and a sudden longing for a riot of purely English colour assailed him.

After that, Everard gave the world that epic painting of a public house – *Romance*; the black street with rain falling – the half-open door, the lights and shining glasses, the little foxy-faced man passing through the doorway, small, mean, insignificant, with lips parted and eyes eager, passing in to forget.

Agatha Christie

On the strength of these two pictures Everard was acclaimed as a painter of 'working men'. He had his niche. But he refused to stay in it. His third and most brilliant work, a full-length portrait of Sir Rufus Herschman. The famous scientist is painted against a background of retorts and crucibles and laboratory shelves. The whole has what may be called a Cubist effect, but the lines of perspective run strangely.

And now he had completed his fourth work – a portrait of his wife. We had been invited to see and criticize. Everard himself scowled and looked out of the window; Isobel Loring moved amongst the guests, talking technique with unerring accuracy.

We made comments. We had to. We praised the painting of the pink satin. The treatment of that, we said, was really marvellous. Nobody had painted satin in quite that way before.

Mrs Lemprière, who is one of the most intelligent art critics I know, took me aside almost at once.

'Georgie,' she said, 'what has he done to himself? The thing's dead. It's smooth. It's – oh! it's damnable.'

'Portrait of a Lady in Pink Satin?' I suggested.

'Exactly. And yet the technique's perfect. And the care! There's enough work there for sixteen pictures.'

'Too much work?' I suggested.

'Perhaps that's it. If there ever was anything there,

he's killed it. An extremely beautiful woman in a pink satin dress. Why not a coloured photograph?'

'Why not?' I agreed. 'Do you suppose he knows?'

'Don't you see the man's on edge? It comes, I daresay, of mixing up sentiment and business. He's put his whole soul into painting Isobel, because she is Isobel, and in sparing her, he's lost her. He's been too kind. You've got to – to destroy the flesh before you can get at the soul sometimes.'

I nodded reflectively. Sir Rufus Herschman had not been flattered physically, but Everard had succeeded in putting on the canvas a personality that was unforgettable.

'And Isobel's got such a very forceful personality,' continued Mrs Lemprière.

'Perhaps Everard can't paint women,' I said.

'Perhaps not,' said Mrs Lemprière thoughtfully. 'Yes, that may be the explanation.'

And it was then, with her usual genius for accuracy, that she pulled out a canvas that was leaning with its face to the wall. There were about eight of them, stacked carelessly. It was pure chance that Mrs Lemprière selected the one she did – but as I said before, these things happen with Mrs Lemprière.

'Ah!' said Mrs Lemprière as she turned it to the light.

It was unfinished, a mere rough sketch. The woman, or girl – she was not, I thought, more than twenty-five or six – was leaning forward, her chin on her hand. Two things struck me at once: the extraordinary vitality of the picture and the amazing cruelty of it. Everard had painted with a vindictive brush. The attitude even was a cruel one – it had brought out every awkwardness, every sharp angle, every crudity. It was a study in brown – brown dress, brown background, brown eyes – wistful, eager eyes. Eagerness was, indeed, the prevailing note of it.

Mrs Lemprière looked at it for some minutes in silence. Then she called to Everard.

'Alan,' she said. 'Come here. Who's this?'

Everard came over obediently. I saw the sudden flash of annoyance that he could not quite hide.

'That's only a daub,' he said. 'I don't suppose I shall ever finish it.'

'Who is she?' said Mrs Lemprière.

Everard was clearly unwilling to answer, and his unwillingness was as meat and drink to Mrs Lemprière, who always believes the worst on principle.

'A friend of mine. A Miss Jane Haworth.'

'I've never met her here,' said Mrs Lemprière.

'She doesn't come to these shows.' He paused a minute, then added: 'She's Winnie's godmother.'

Winnie was his little daughter, aged five.

'Really?' said Mrs Lemprière. 'Where does she live?'

'Battersea. A flat.'

'Really,' said Mrs Lemprière again, and then added: 'And what has she ever done to you?'

'To me?'

'To you. To make you so – ruthless.'

'Oh, that!' he laughed. 'Well, you know, she's not a beauty. I can't make her one out of friendship, can I?'

'You've done the opposite,' said Mrs Lemprière. 'You've caught hold of every defect of hers and exaggerated it and twisted it. You've tried to make her ridiculous – but you haven't succeeded, my child. That portrait, if you finish it, will live.'

Everard looked annoyed.

'It's not bad,' he said lightly, 'for a sketch, that is. But, of course, it's not a patch on Isobel's portrait. That's far and away the best thing I've ever done.'

He said the last words defiantly and aggressively. Neither of us answered.

'Far and away the best thing,' he repeated.

Some of the others had drawn near us. They, too, caught sight of the sketch. There were exclamations, comments. The atmosphere began to brighten up.

It was in this way that I first heard of Jane Haworth. Later, I was to meet her – twice. I was to hear details of her life from one of her most intimate friends. I was to learn much from Alan Everard himself. Now that they are both dead, I think it is time to contradict some of the stories Mrs Lemprière is busily spreading abroad.

Call some of my story invention if you will – it is not far from the truth.

II

When the guests had left, Alan Everard turned the portrait of Jane Haworth with its face to the wall again. Isobel came down the room and stood beside him.

'A success, do you think?' she asked thoughtfully. 'Or – not quite a success?'

'The portrait?' he asked quickly.

'No, silly, the party. Of course the portrait's a success.'

'It's the best thing I've done,' Everard declared aggressively.

'We're getting on,' said Isobel. 'Lady Charmington wants you to paint her.'

'Oh, Lord!' He frowned. 'I'm not a fashionable portrait painter, you know.'

'You will be. You'll get to the top of the tree.'

'That's not the tree I want to get to the top of.'

'But, Alan dear, that's the way to make mints of money.'

'Who wants mints of money?'

'Perhaps I do,' she said smiling.

At once he felt apologetic, ashamed. If she had not

married him she could have had her mints of money. And she needed it. A certain amount of luxury was her proper setting.

'We've not done so badly just lately,' he said wistfully.

'No, indeed; but the bills are coming in rather fast.'

Bills – always bills!

He walked up and down.

'Oh, hang it! I don't want to paint Lady Charmington,' he burst out, rather like a petulant child.

Isobel smiled a little. She stood by the fire without moving. Alan stopped his restless pacing and came nearer to her. What was there in her, in her stillness, her inertia, that drew him – drew him like a magnet? How beautiful she was – her arms like sculptured white marble, the pure gold of her hair, her lips – red full lips.

He kissed them – felt them fasten on his own. Did anything else matter? What was there in Isobel that soothed you, that took all your cares from you? She drew you into her own beautiful inertia and held you there, quiet and content. Poppy and mandragora; you drifted there, on a dark lake, asleep.

'I'll do Lady Charmington,' he said presently. 'What does it matter? I shall be bored – but after all, painters must eat. There's Mr Pots the painter, Mrs Pots the painter's wife, and Miss Pots the painter's daughter – all needing sustenance.'

'Absurd boy!' said Isobel. 'Talking of our daughter – you ought to go and see Jane some time. She was here yesterday, and said she hadn't seen you for months.'

'Jane was here?'

'Yes – to see Winnie.'

Alan brushed Winnie aside.

'Did she see the picture of you?'

'Yes.'

'What did she think of it?'

'She said it was splendid.'

'Oh!'

He frowned, lost in thought.

'Mrs Lemprière suspects you of a guilty passion for Jane, I think,' remarked Isobel. 'Her nose twitched a good deal.'

'That woman!' said Alan, with deep disgust. 'That woman! What wouldn't she think? What doesn't she think?'

'Well, *I* don't think,' said Isobel, smiling. 'So go and see Jane soon.'

Alan looked across at her. She was sitting now on a low couch by the fire. Her face was half turned away, the smile still lingered on her lips. And at that moment he felt bewildered, confused, as though a mist had formed round him, and, suddenly parting, had given him a glimpse into a strange country.

Something said to him: 'Why does she want you to

go and see Jane? There's a reason.' Because with Isobel, there was bound to be a reason. There was no impulse in Isobel, only calculation.

'Do you like Jane?' he asked suddenly.

'She's a dear,' said Isobel.

'Yes, but do you really like her?'

'Of course. She's so devoted to Winnie. By the way, she wants to carry Winnie off to the seaside next week. You don't mind, do you? It will leave us free for Scotland.'

'It will be extraordinarily convenient.'

It would, indeed, be just that. Extraordinarily convenient. He looked across at Isobel with a sudden suspicion. Had she *asked* Jane? Jane was so easily imposed upon.

Isobel got up and went out of the room, humming to herself. Oh, well, it didn't matter. Anyway, he would go and see Jane.

III

Jane Haworth lived at the top of a block of mansion flats overlooking Battersea Park. When Everard had climbed four flights of stairs and pressed the bell, he felt annoyed with Jane. Why couldn't she live somewhere more get-at-able? When, not having obtained an answer, he had pressed the bell three times, his annoyance had grown greater. Why couldn't she keep someone capable of answering the door?

Suddenly it opened, and Jane herself stood in the doorway. She was flushed.

'Where's Alice?' asked Everard, without any attempt at greeting.

'Well, I'm afraid – I mean – she's not well today.'

'Drunk, you mean?' said Everard grimly.

What a pity that Jane was such an inveterate liar.

'I suppose that's it,' said Jane reluctantly.

'Let me see her.'

He strode into the flat. Jane followed him with disarming meekness. He found the delinquent Alice in the kitchen. There was no doubt whatever as to her condition. He followed Jane into the sitting-room in grim silence.

'You'll have to get rid of that woman,' he said. 'I told you so before.'

'I know you did, Alan, but I can't do that. You forget, her husband's in prison.'

'Where he ought to be,' said Everard. 'How often has that woman been drunk in the three months you've had her?'

'Not so very many times; three or four perhaps. She gets depressed, you know.'

'Three or four! Nine or ten would be nearer the

mark. How does she cook? Rottenly. Is she the least assistance or comfort to you in this flat? None whatever. For God's sake, get rid of her tomorrow morning and engage a girl who is of some use.'

Jane looked at him unhappily.

'You won't,' said Everard gloomily, sinking into a big armchair. 'You're such an impossibly sentimental creature. What's this I hear about your taking Winnie to the seaside? Who suggested it, you or Isobel?'

Jane said very quickly: 'I did, of course.'

'Jane,' said Everard, 'if you would only learn to speak the truth, I should be quite fond of you. Sit down, and for goodness' sake don't tell any more lies for at least ten minutes.'

'Oh, Alan!' said Jane, and sat down.

The painter examined her critically for a minute or two. Mrs Lemprière – that woman – had been quite right. He had been cruel in his handling of Jane. Jane was almost, if not quite, beautiful. The long lines of her body were pure Greek. It was that eager anxiety of hers to please that made her awkward. He had seized on that – exaggerated it – had sharpened the line of her slightly pointed chin, flung her body into an ugly poise.

Why? Why was it impossible for him to be five minutes in the room with Jane without feeling violent irritation against her rising up in him? Say what you

191

would, Jane was a dear, but irritating. He was never soothed and at peace with her as he was with Isobel. And yet Jane was so anxious to please, so willing to agree with all he said, but alas! so transparently unable to conceal her real feelings.

He looked round the room. Typically Jane. Some lovely things, pure gems, that piece of Battersea enamel, for instance, and there next to it, an atrocity of a vase hand-painted with roses.

He picked the latter up.

'Would you be very angry, Jane, if I pitched this out of the window?'

'Oh! Alan, you mustn't.'

'What do you want with all this trash? You've plenty of taste if you care to use it. Mixing things up!'

'I know, Alan. It isn't that I don't *know*. But people give me things. That vase – Miss Bates brought it back from Margate – and she's so poor, and has to scrape, and it must have cost her quite a lot – for her, you know, and she thought I'd be so pleased. I simply had to put it in a good place.'

Everard said nothing. He went on looking round the room. There were one or two etchings on the walls – there were also a number of photographs of babies. Babies, whatever their mothers may think, do not always photograph well. Any of Jane's friends who acquired babies hurried to send photographs of them to her, expecting these tokens to be cherished. Jane had duly cherished them.

'Who's this little horror?' asked Everard, inspecting a pudgy addition with a squint. 'I've not seen him before.'

'It's a her,' said Jane. 'Mary Carrington's new baby.'

'Poor Mary Carrington,' said Everard. 'I suppose you'll pretend that you like having that atrocious infant squinting at you all day?'

Jane's chin shot out.

'She's a lovely baby. Mary is a very old friend of mine.'

'Loyal Jane,' said Everard smiling at her. 'So Isobel landed you with Winnie, did she?'

'Well, she did say you wanted to go to Scotland, and I jumped at it. You will let me have Winnie, won't you? I've been wondering if you would let her come to me for ages, but I haven't liked to ask.'

'Oh, you can have her – but it's awfully good of you.'

'Then that's all right,' said Jane happily.

Everard lit a cigarette.

'Isobel show you the new portrait?' he asked rather indistinctly.

'She did.'

'What did you think of it?'

Jane's answer came quickly – too quickly:

'It's perfectly splendid. Absolutely splendid.'

Alan sprang suddenly to his feet. The hand that held the cigarette shook.

'Damn you, Jane, don't lie to me!'

'But, Alan, I'm sure, it *is* perfectly splendid.'

'Haven't you learnt by now, Jane, that I know every tone of your voice? You lie to me like a hatter so as not to hurt my feelings, I suppose. Why can't you be honest? Do you think I want you to tell me a thing is splendid when I know as well as you do that it's not? The damned thing's dead – dead. There's no life in it – nothing behind, nothing but surface, damned smooth surface. I've cheated myself all along – yes, even this afternoon. I came along to you to find out. Isobel doesn't know. But you know, you always do know. I knew you'd tell me it was good – you've no moral sense about that sort of thing. But I can tell by the tone of your voice. When I showed you *Romance* you didn't say anything at all – you held your breath and gave a sort of gasp.'

'Alan . . .'

Everard gave her no chance to speak. Jane was producing the effect upon him he knew so well. Strange that so gentle a creature could stir him to such furious anger.

'You think I've lost the power, perhaps,' he said angrily, 'but I haven't. I can do work every bit as good as *Romance* – better, perhaps. I'll show you, Jane Haworth.'

He fairly rushed out of the flat. Walking rapidly, he crossed through the Park and over Albert Bridge. He was still tingling all over with irritation and baffled rage. Jane, indeed! What did *she* know about painting? What was *her* opinion worth? Why should he care? But he did care. He wanted to paint something that would make Jane gasp. Her mouth would open just a little, and her cheeks would flush red. She would look first at the picture and then at him. She wouldn't say anything at all probably.

In the middle of the bridge he saw the picture he was going to paint. It came to him from nowhere at all, out of the blue. He saw it, there in the air, or was it in his head?

A little, dingy curio shop, rather dark and musty-looking. Behind the counter a Jew – a small Jew with cunning eyes. In front of him the customer, a big man, sleek, well fed, opulent, bloated, a great jowl on him. Above them, on a shelf, a bust of white marble. The light there, on the boy's marble face, the deathless beauty of old Greece, scornful, unheeding of sale and barter. The Jew, the rich collector, the Greek boy's head. He saw them all.

'*The Connoisseur*, that's what I'll call it,' muttered Alan Everard, stepping off the kerb and just missing being annihilated by a passing bus. 'Yes, *The Connoisseur*. I'll *show* Jane.'

When he arrived home, he passed straight into the studio. Isobel found him there, sorting out canvases.

'Alan, don't forget we're dining with the Marches –'

Everard shook his head impatiently.

'Damn the Marches. I'm going to work. I've got hold of something, but I must get it fixed – fixed at once on the canvas before it goes. Ring them up. Tell them I'm dead.'

Isobel looked at him thoughtfully for a moment or two, and then went out. She understood the art of living with a genius very thoroughly. She went to the telephone and made some plausible excuse.

She looked round her, yawning a little. Then she sat down at her desk and began to write.

'*Dear Jane,*

Many thanks for your cheque received today. You are good to your godchild. A hundred pounds will do all sorts of things. Children are a terrible expense. You are so fond of Winnie that I felt I was not doing wrong in coming to you for help. Alan, like all geniuses, can only work at what he wants to work at – and unfortunately that doesn't always keep the pot boiling. Hope to see you soon.

Yours, Isobel'

When *The Connoisseur* was finished, some months later, Alan invited Jane to come and see it. The thing was not quite as he had conceived it – that was impossible to hope for – but it was near enough. He felt the glow of the creator. He had made this thing and it was good.

Jane did not this time tell him it was splendid. The colour crept into her cheeks and her lips parted. She looked at Alan, and he saw in her eyes that which he wished to see. Jane knew.

He walked on air. He had shown Jane!

The picture off his mind, he began to notice his immediate surroundings once more.

Winnie had benefited enormously from her fortnight at the seaside, but it struck him that her clothes were very shabby. He said so to Isobel.

'Alan! You who never notice anything! But I like children to be simply dressed – I hate them all fussed up.'

'There's a difference between simplicity and darns and patches.'

Isobel said nothing, but she got Winnie a new frock.

Two days later Alan was struggling with income tax returns. His own pass book lay in front of him. He was hunting through Isobel's desk for hers when Winnie danced into the room with a disreputable doll.

'Daddy, I've got a riddle. Can you guess it? "Within a wall as white as milk, within a curtain soft as silk, bathed in a sea of crystal clear, a golden apple doth appear." Guess what that is?'

'Your mother,' said Alan absently. He was still hunting.

'Daddy!' Winnie gave a scream of laughter. 'It's an *egg*. Why did you think it was mummy?'

Alan smiled too.

'I wasn't really listening,' he said. 'And the words sounded like mummy, somehow.'

A wall as white as milk. A curtain. Crystal. The golden apple. Yes, it did suggest Isobel to him. Curious things, words.

He had found the pass book now. He ordered Winnie peremptorily from the room. Ten minutes later he looked up, startled by a sharp exclamation.

'Alan!'

'Hullo, Isobel. I didn't hear you come in. Look here, I can't make out these items in your pass book.'

'What business had you to touch my pass book?'

He stared at her, astonished. She was angry. He had never seen her angry before.

'I had no idea you would mind.'

'I do mind – very much indeed. You have no business to touch my things.'

Alan suddenly became angry too.

'I apologize. But since I have touched your things, perhaps you will explain one or two entries that puzzle me. As far as I can see, nearly five hundred pounds has been paid into your account this year which I cannot check. Where does it come from?'

Isobel had recovered her temper. She sank into a chair.

'You needn't be so solemn about it, Alan,' she said lightly. 'It isn't the wages of sin, or anything like that.'

'Where did this money come from?'

'From a woman. A friend of yours. It's not mine at all. It's for Winnie.'

'Winnie? Do you mean – this money came from Jane?'

Isobel nodded.

'She's devoted to the child – can't do enough for her.'

'Yes, but – surely the money ought to have been invested for Winnie.'

'Oh! it isn't that sort of thing at all. It's for current expenses, clothes and all that.'

Alan said nothing. He was thinking of Winnie's frocks – all darns and patches.

'Your account's overdrawn, too, Isobel?'

'Is it? That's always happening to me.'

'Yes, but that five hundred –'

'My dear Alan, I've spent it on Winnie in the way that seemed best to me. I can assure you Jane is quite satisfied.'

Alan was *not* satisfied. Yet such was the power of Isobel's calm that he said nothing more. After all, Isobel was careless in money matters. She hadn't meant to use for herself money given to her for the child. A receipted bill came that day addressed by a mistake to Mr Everard. It was from a dressmaker in Hanover Square and was for two hundred odd pounds. He gave it to Isobel without a word. She glanced over it, smiled, and said:

'Poor boy, I suppose it seems an awful lot to you, but one really *must* be more or less clothed.'

The next day he went to see Jane.

Jane was irritating and elusive as usual. He wasn't to bother. Winnie was her godchild. Women understood these things, men didn't. Of course she didn't want Winnie to have five hundred pounds' worth of frocks. Would he please leave it to her and Isobel? They understood each other perfectly.

Alan went away in a state of growing dissatisfaction. He knew perfectly well that he had shirked the one question he really wished to ask. He wanted to say: 'Has Isobel ever asked you for money for Winnie?' He didn't say it because he was afraid that Jane might not lie well enough to deceive him.

But he was worried. Jane was poor. He knew she was poor. She mustn't – mustn't denude herself. He made up his mind to speak to Isobel. Isobel was calm and reassuring. Of course she wouldn't let Jane spend more than she could afford.

IV

A month later Jane died.

It was influenza, followed by pneumonia. She made Alan Everard her executor and left all she had to Winnie. But it wasn't very much.

It was Alan's task to go through Jane's papers. She left a record there that was clear to follow – numerous evidences of acts of kindness, begging letters, grateful letters.

And lastly, he found her diary. With it was a scrap of paper:

'To be read after my death by Alan Everard. He has often reproached me with not speaking the truth. The truth is all here.'

So he came to know at last, finding the one place where Jane had dared to be honest. It was a record, very simple and unforced, of her love for him.

There was very little sentiment about it – no fine language. But there was no blinking of facts.

'I know you are often irritated by me,' she had written. 'Everything I do or say seems to make you angry sometimes. I do not know why this should be, for I try so hard to please you; but I do believe, all the same, that I mean something real to you. One isn't angry with the people who don't count.'

It was not Jane's fault that Alan found other matters. Jane was loyal – but she was also untidy; she filled her drawers too full. She had, shortly before her death, burnt carefully all Isobel's letters. The one Alan found was wedged behind a drawer. When he had read it, the meaning of certain cabalistic signs on the counterfoils of Jane's cheque book became clear to him. In this particular letter Isobel had hardly troubled to keep up the pretence of the money being required for Winnie.

Alan sat in front of the desk staring with unseeing eyes out of the window for a long time. Finally he slipped the cheque book into his pocket and left the flat. He walked back to Chelsea, conscious of an anger that grew rapidly stronger.

Isobel was out when he got back, and he was sorry. He had so clearly in his mind what he wanted to say. Instead, he went up to the studio and pulled out the unfinished portrait of Jane. He set it on an easel near the portrait of Isobel in pink satin.

The Lemprière woman had been right; there was life in Jane's portrait. He looked at her, the eager eyes, the beauty that he had tried so unsuccessfully to deny her. That was Jane – the aliveness, more than anything else, was Jane. She was, he thought, the most alive person he had ever met, so much so, that even now he could not think of her as dead.

And he thought of his other pictures – *Colour*, *Romance*, Sir Rufus Herschman. They had all, in a way, been pictures of Jane. She had kindled the spark for each one of them – had sent him away fuming and fretting – to *show* her! And now? Jane was dead. Would he ever paint a picture – a real picture – again? He looked again at the eager face on the canvas. Perhaps. Jane wasn't very far away.

A sound made him wheel round. Isobel had come into the studio. She was dressed for dinner in a straight white gown that showed up the pure gold of her hair.

She stopped dead and checked the words on her lips. Eyeing him warily, she went over to the divan and sat down. She had every appearance of calm.

Alan took the cheque book from his pocket.

'I've been going through Jane's papers.'

'Yes?'

He tried to imitate her calm, to keep his voice from shaking.

'For the last four years she's been supplying you with money.'

'Yes. For Winnie.'

'No, not for Winnie,' shouted Everard. 'You pretended, both of you, that it was for Winnie, but you both knew that that wasn't so. Do you realize that

Jane has been selling her securities, living from hand to mouth, to supply you with clothes – clothes that you didn't really need?'

Isobel never took her eyes from his face. She settled her body more comfortably on the cushions as a white Persian cat might do.

'I can't help it if Jane denuded herself more than she should have done,' she said. 'I supposed she could afford the money. She was always crazy about you – I could see that, of course. Some wives would have kicked up a fuss about the way you were always rushing off to see her, and spending hours there. I didn't.'

'No,' said Alan, very white in the face. 'You made her pay instead.'

'You are saying very offensive things, Alan. Be careful.'

'Aren't they true? Why did you find it so easy to get money out of Jane?'

'Not for love of me, certainly. It must have been for love of you.'

'That's just what it was,' said Alan simply. 'She paid for my freedom – freedom to work in my own way. So long as you had a sufficiency of money, you'd leave me alone – not badger me to paint a crowd of awful women.'

Isobel said nothing.

'Well?' cried Alan angrily.

Her quiescence infuriated him.

Isobel was looking at the floor. Presently she raised her head and said quietly:

'Come here, Alan.'

She touched the divan at her side. Uneasily, unwillingly, he came and sat there, not looking at her. But he knew that he was afraid.

'Alan,' said Isobel presently.

'Well?'

He was irritable, nervous.

'All that you say may be true. It doesn't matter. I'm like that. I want things – clothes, money, *you*. *Jane's dead*, Alan.'

'What do you mean?'

'Jane's dead. You belong to me altogether now. You never did before – not quite.'

He looked at her – saw the light in her eyes, acquisitive, possessive – was revolted, yet fascinated.

'Now you shall be all mine.'

He understood Isobel then as he had never understood her before.

'You want me as a slave? I'm to paint what you tell me to paint, live as you tell me to live, be dragged at your chariot wheels.'

'Put it like that if you please. What are words?'

He felt her arms round his neck, white, smooth, firm as a wall. Words danced through his brain. 'A wall as

205

white as milk.' Already he was inside the wall. Could he still escape? Did he want to escape?

He heard her voice close against his ear – poppy and mandragora.

'What else is there to live for? Isn't this enough? Love – happiness – success – love –'

The wall was growing up all round him now – 'the curtain soft as silk', the curtain wrapping him round, stifling him a little, but so soft, so sweet! Now they were drifting together, at peace, out on the crystal sea. The wall was very high now, shutting out all those other things – those dangerous, disturbing things that hurt – that always hurt. Out on the sea of crystal, the golden apple between their hands.

The light faded from Jane's picture.

Afterword

Like many of Christie's early short stories, 'Within a Wall', first published in the *Royal Magazine* in October 1925, is somewhat ambiguous. The concluding remarks about the encircling white walls *can* be taken as what they appear to be, a description of the arms of Isobel Loring as they wind around Alan Everard, but how else might the phrase be interpreted? There is the obscure closing reference to 'The golden apple within their hands' – whose hands, and what does the 'golden apple' symbolize? Is there perhaps a darker significance to Alan's earlier misunderstanding of Winnie's riddle? Is he in fact strangling his wife at the end of the story? Or, given that 'the light' is fading from Jane's picture at the end, is the reader supposed to understand that Alan has forgotten her and forgiven Isobel? And what of his own death? Christie does not explain the circumstances, only noting that it has led to unkind rumours which the narrator of the story is seeking to scotch.

The story is also based around one of the most common motifs in the work of Agatha Christie, the eternal triangle. This features in various works, including the similarly structured Poirot novels *Death on the Nile* (1937) and *Evil Under the Sun* (1941) and in short stories like 'The Bloodstained Pavement', collected in *The Thirteen Problems* (1932). In *A Talent to Deceive* (1980), unquestionably the finest critique of her writing, Robert Barnard describes how Christie uses this and other commonplace themes as one of her 'strategies of deception', tricking readers into misdirecting their sympathy (and suspicions) by playing on their expectations. She also adopted similar tactics in her stage plays, most notably in *The Mousetrap* (1952).

The Mystery of
The Baghdad Chest

The words made a catchy headline, and I said as much to my friend, Hercule Poirot. I knew none of the parties. My interest was merely the dispassionate one of the man in the street. Poirot agreed.

'Yes, it has a flavour of the Oriental, of the mysterious. The chest may very well have been a sham Jacobean one from the Tottenham Court Road; none the less the reporter who thought of naming it the Baghdad Chest was happily inspired. The word "mystery" is also thoughtfully placed in juxtaposition, though I understand there is very little mystery about the case.'

'Exactly. It is all rather horrible and macabre, but it is not mysterious.'

'Horrible and macabre,' repeated Poirot thoughtfully.

'The whole idea is revolting,' I said, rising to my feet and pacing up and down the room. 'The murderer kills this man – his friend – shoves him into the chest, and half an hour later is dancing in that same room with the wife of his victim. Think! If she had imagined for one moment –'

'True,' said Poirot thoughtfully. 'That much-vaunted possession, a woman's intuition – it does not seem to have been working.'

'The party seems to have gone off very merrily,' I said with a slight shiver. 'And all that time, as they danced and played poker, there was a dead man in the room with them. One could write a play about such an idea.'

'It has been done,' said Poirot. 'But console yourself, Hastings,' he added kindly. 'Because a theme has been used once, there is no reason why it should not be used again. Compose your drama.'

I had picked up the paper and was studying the rather blurred reproduction of a photograph.

'She must be a beautiful woman,' I said slowly. 'Even from this, one gets an idea.'

Below the picture ran the inscription:

A recent portrait of Mrs Clayton,
the wife of the murdered man

Poirot took the paper from me.

'Yes,' he said. 'She is beautiful. Doubtless she is of those born to trouble the souls of men.'

He handed the paper back to me with a sigh.

'*Dieu merci*, I am not of an ardent temperament. It has saved me from many embarrassments. I am duly thankful.'

I do not remember that we discussed the case further. Poirot displayed no special interest in it at the time. The facts were so clear, and there was so little ambiguity about them, that discussion seemed merely futile.

Mr and Mrs Clayton and Major Rich were friends of fairly long-standing. On the day in question, the tenth of March, the Claytons had accepted an invitation to spend the evening with Major Rich. At about seven-thirty, however, Clayton explained to another friend, a Major Curtiss, with whom he was having a drink, that he had been unexpectedly called to Scotland and was leaving by the eight o'clock train.

'I'll just have time to drop in and explain to old Jack,' went on Clayton. 'Marguerita is going, of course. I'm sorry about it, but Jack will understand how it is.'

Mr Clayton was as good as his word. He arrived at Major Rich's rooms about twenty to eight. The major was out at the time, but his manservant, who knew Mr Clayton well, suggested that he come in and wait. Mr Clayton said that he had no time, but that he would come in and write a note. He added that he was on his way to catch a train.

Agatha Christie

The valet accordingly showed him into the sitting-room.

About five minutes later Major Rich, who must have let himself in without the valet hearing him, opened the door of the sitting-room, called his man and told him to go out and get some cigarettes. On his return the man brought them to his master, who was then alone in the sitting-room. The man naturally concluded that Mr Clayton had left.

The guests arrived shortly afterwards. They comprised Mrs Clayton, Major Curtiss and a Mr and Mrs Spence. The evening was spent dancing to the phonograph and playing poker. The guests left shortly after midnight.

The following morning, on coming to do the sitting-room, the valet was startled to find a deep stain discolouring the carpet below and in front of a piece of furniture which Major Rich had brought from the East and which was called the Baghdad Chest.

Instinctively the valet lifted the lid of the chest and was horrified to find inside the doubled-up body of a man who had been stabbed to the heart.

Terrified, the man ran out of the flat and fetched the nearest policeman. The dead man proved to be Mr Clayton. The arrest of Major Rich followed very shortly afterward. The major's defence, it was understood, consisted of a sturdy denial of everything. He had not seen Mr Clayton the preceding evening and the first he had heard of his going to Scotland had been from Mrs Clayton.

Such were the bald facts of the case. Innuendoes and suggestions naturally abounded. The close friendship and intimacy of Major Rich and Mrs Clayton were so stressed that only a fool could fail to read between the lines. The motive for the crime was plainly indicated.

Long experience has taught me to make allowance for baseless calumny. The motive suggested might, for all the evidence, be entirely non-existent. Some quite other reason might have precipitated the issue. But one thing did stand out clearly – that Rich was the murderer.

As I say, the matter might have rested there, had it not happened that Poirot and I were due at a party given by Lady Chatterton that night.

Poirot, whilst bemoaning social engagements and declaring a passion for solitude, really enjoyed these affairs enormously. To be made a fuss of and treated as a lion suited him down to the ground.

On occasions he positively purred! I have seen him blandly receiving the most outrageous compliments as no more than his due, and uttering the most blatantly conceited remarks, such as I can hardly bear to set down.

Sometimes he would argue with me on the subject.

'But, my friend, I am not an Anglo-Saxon. Why should I play the hypocrite? *Si, si*, that is what you do, all of you. The airman who has made a difficult flight, the tennis champion – they look down their noses, they mutter inaudibly that "it is nothing". But do they really think that themselves? Not for a moment. They would admire the exploit in someone else. So, being reasonable men, they admire it in themselves. But their training prevents them from saying so. Me, I am not like that. The talents that I possess – I would salute them in another. As it happens, in my own particular line, there is no one to touch me. *C'est dommage!* As it is, I admit freely and without hypocrisy that I am a great man. I have the order, the method and the psychology in an unusual degree. I am, in fact, Hercule Poirot! Why should I turn red and stammer and mutter into my chin that really I am very stupid? It would not be true.'

'There is certainly only one Hercule Poirot,' I agreed – not without a spice of malice of which, fortunately, Poirot remained quite oblivious.

Lady Chatterton was one of Poirot's most ardent admirers. Starting from the mysterious conduct of a Pekingese, he had unravelled a chain which led to a noted burglar and housebreaker. Lady Chatterton had been loud in his praises ever since.

To see Poirot at a party was a great sight. His faultless evening clothes, the exquisite set of his white tie, the exact symmetry of his hair parting, the sheen of pomade on his hair, and the tortured splendour of his famous moustaches – all combined to paint the perfect picture of an inveterate dandy. It was hard, at these moments, to take the little man seriously.

It was about half-past eleven when Lady Chatterton, bearing down upon us, whisked Poirot neatly out of an admiring group, and carried him off – I need hardly say, with myself in tow.

'I want you to go into my little room upstairs,' said Lady Chatterton rather breathlessly as soon as she was out of earshot of her other guests. 'You know where it is, M. Poirot. You'll find someone there who needs your help very badly – and you will help her, I know. She's one of my dearest friends – so don't say no.'

Energetically leading the way as she talked, Lady Chatterton flung open a door, exclaiming as she did so, 'I've got him, Marguerita darling. And he'll do anything you want. You *will* help Mrs Clayton, won't you, M. Poirot?'

And taking the answer for granted, she withdrew with the same energy that characterized all her movements.

Mrs Clayton had been sitting in a chair by the window. She rose now and came toward us. Dressed in deep mourning, the dull black showed up her fair colouring. She was a singularly lovely woman, and there was about her a simple childlike candour which made her charm quite irresistible.

'Alice Chatterton is so kind,' she said. 'She arranged this. She said you would help me, M. Poirot. Of course I don't know whether you will or not – but I hope you will.'

She had held out her hand and Poirot had taken it. He held it now for a moment or two while he stood scrutinizing her closely. There was nothing ill-bred in his manner of doing it. It was more the kind but searching look that a famous consultant gives a new patient as the latter is ushered into his presence.

'Are you sure, madame,' he said at last, 'that I can help you?'

'Alice says so.'

'Yes, but I am asking you, madame.'

A little flush rose to her cheeks.

'I don't know what you mean.'

'What is it, madame, that you want me to do?'

'You – you – know who I am?' she asked.

'Assuredly.'

'Then you can guess what it is I am asking you to do, M. Poirot – Captain Hastings' – I was gratified that she realized my identity – 'Major Rich did *not* kill my husband.'

'Why not?'

'I beg your pardon?'

Poirot smiled at her slight discomfiture.

'I said, "Why not?"' he repeated.

'I'm not sure that I understand.'

'Yet it is very simple. The police – the lawyers – they will all ask the same question: Why did Major Rich kill M. Clayton? I ask the opposite. I ask you, madame, why did Major Rich *not* kill Mr Clayton.'

'You mean – why I'm so sure? Well, but I *know*. I know Major Rich so well.'

'You know Major Rich so well,' repeated Poirot tonelessly.

The colour flamed into her cheeks.

'Yes, that's what they'll say – what they'll think! Oh, I know!'

'*C'est vrai.* That is what they will ask you about – how well you knew Major Rich. Perhaps you will speak the truth, perhaps you will lie. It is very necessary for a woman to lie, it is a good weapon. But there are three people, madame, to whom a woman should speak the truth. To her Father Confessor, to her hairdresser and to her private detective – if she trusts him. Do you trust me, madame?'

Marguerita Clayton drew a deep breath. 'Yes,' she said. 'I do. I must,' she added rather childishly.

'Then, how well do you know Major Rich?'

She looked at him for a moment in silence, then she raised her chin defiantly.

'I will answer your question. I loved Jack from the first moment I saw him – two years ago. Lately I think – I believe – he has come to love me. But he has never said so.'

'*Épatant!*' said Poirot. 'You have saved me a good quarter of an hour by coming to the point without beating the bush. You have the good sense. Now your husband – did he suspect your feelings?'

'I don't know,' said Marguerita slowly. 'I thought – lately – that he might. His manner has been different . . . But that may have been merely my fancy.'

'Nobody else knew?'

'I do not think so.'

'And – pardon me, madame – you did not love your husband?'

There were, I think, very few women who would have answered that question as simply as this woman did. They would have tried to explain their feelings.

Marguerita Clayton said quite simply: 'No.'

'*Bien.* Now we know where we are. According to you, madame, Major Rich did not kill your husband, but you realize that all the evidence points to his having done so. Are you aware, privately, of any flaw in that evidence?'

'No. I know nothing.'

'When did your husband first inform you of his visit to Scotland?'

'Just after lunch. He said it was a bore, but he'd have to go. Something to do with land values, he said it was.'

'And after that?'

'He went out – to his club, I think. I – I didn't see him again.'

'Now as to Major Rich – what was his manner that evening? Just as usual?'

'Yes, I think so.'

'You are not sure?'

Marguerita wrinkled her brows.

'He was – a little constrained. With me – not with the others. But I thought I knew why that was. You understand? I am sure the constraint or – or – absent-mindedness perhaps describes it better – had nothing to do with Edward. He was surprised to hear that Edward had gone to Scotland, but not unduly so.'

'And nothing else unusual occurs to you in connection with that evening?'

Marguerita thought.

'No, nothing whatever.'

'You – noticed the chest?'

She shook her head with a little shiver.

'I don't even remember it – or what it was like. We played poker most of the evening.'

'Who won?'

'Major Rich. I had very bad luck, and so did Major

Curtiss. The Spences won a little, but Major Rich was the chief winner.'

'The party broke up – when?'

'About half-past twelve, I think. We all left together.'

'Ah!'

Poirot remained silent, lost in thought.

'I wish I could be more helpful to you,' said Mrs Clayton. 'I seem to be able to tell you so little.'

'About the present – yes. What about the past, madame?'

'The past?'

'Yes. Have there not been incidents?'

She flushed.

'You mean that dreadful little man who shot himself. It wasn't my fault, M. Poirot. Indeed it wasn't.'

'It was not precisely of that incident that I was thinking.'

'That ridiculous duel? But Italians do fight duels. I was so thankful the man wasn't killed.'

'It must have been a relief to you,' agreed Poirot gravely.

She was looking at him doubtfully. He rose and took her hand in his.

'I shall not fight a duel for you, madame,' he said. 'But I will do what you have asked me. I will discover the truth. And let us hope that your instincts are correct – that the truth will help and not harm you.'

Our first interview was with Major Curtiss. He was a man of about forty, of soldierly build, with very dark hair and a bronzed face. He had known the Claytons for some years and Major Rich also. He confirmed the press reports.

Clayton and he had had a drink together at the club just before half-past seven, and Clayton had then announced his intention of looking in on Major Rich on his way to Euston.

'What was Mr Clayton's manner? Was he depressed or cheerful?'

The major considered. He was a slow-spoken man.

'Seemed in fairly good spirits,' he said at last.

'He said nothing about being on bad terms with Major Rich?'

'Good Lord, no. They were pals.'

'He didn't object to – his wife's friendship with Major Rich?'

The major became very red in the face.

'You've been reading those damned newspapers, with their hints and lies. Of course he didn't object. Why, he said to me: "Marguerita's going, of course."'

'I see. Now during the evening – the manner of Major Rich – was that much as usual?'

'I didn't notice any difference.'

'And madame? She, too, was as usual.'

'Well,' he reflected, 'now I come to think of it, she

was a bit quiet. You know, thoughtful and faraway.'

'Who arrived first?'

'The Spences. They were there when I got there. As a matter of fact, I'd called round for Mrs Clayton, but found she'd already started. So I got there a bit late.'

'And how did you amuse yourselves? You danced? You played the cards?'

'A bit of both. Danced first of all.'

'There were five of you?'

'Yes, but that's all right, because I don't dance. I put on the records and the others danced.'

'Who danced most with whom?'

'Well, as a matter of fact the Spences like dancing together. They've got a sort of craze on it – fancy steps and all that.'

'So that Mrs Clayton danced mostly with Major Rich?'

'That's about it.'

'And then you played poker?'

'Yes.'

'And when did you leave?'

'Oh, quite early. A little after midnight.'

'Did you all leave together?'

'Yes. As a matter of fact, we shared a taxi, dropped Mrs Clayton first, then me, and the Spences took it on to Kensington.'

Our next visit was to Mr and Mrs Spence. Only

Mrs Spence was at home, but her account of the evening tallied with that of Major Curtiss except that she displayed a slight acidity concerning Major Rich's luck at cards.

Earlier in the morning Poirot had had a telephone conversation with Inspector Japp of Scotland Yard. As a result we arrived at Major Rich's rooms and found his manservant, Burgoyne, expecting us.

The valet's evidence was very precise and clear.

Mr Clayton had arrived at twenty minutes to eight. Unluckily Major Rich had just that very minute gone out. Mr Clayton had said that he couldn't wait, as he had to catch a train, but he would just scrawl a note. He accordingly went into the sitting-room to do so. Burgoyne had not actually heard his master come in, as he was running the bath, and Major Rich, of course, let himself in with his own key. In his opinion it was about ten minutes later that Major Rich called him and sent him out for cigarettes. No, he had not gone into the sitting-room. Major Rich had stood in the doorway. He had returned with the cigarettes five minutes later and on this occasion he had gone into the sitting-room, which was then empty, save for his master, who was standing by the window smoking. His master had inquired if his bath were ready and on being told it was had proceeded to take it. He, Burgoyne, had not mentioned Mr Clayton, as he assumed that his master had found Mr Clayton there and let him out himself. His master's manner had been precisely the same as usual. He had taken his bath, changed, and shortly after, Mr and Mrs Spence had arrived, to be followed by Major Curtiss and Mrs Clayton.

It had not occurred to him, Burgoyne explained, that Mr Clayton might have left before his master's return. To do so, Mr Clayton would have had to bang the front door behind him and that the valet was sure he would have heard.

Still in the same impersonal manner, Burgoyne proceeded to his finding of the body. For the first time my attention was directed to the fatal chest. It was a good-sized piece of furniture standing against the wall next to the phonograph cabinet. It was made of some dark wood and plentifully studded with brass nails. The lid opened simply enough. I looked in and shivered. Though well scrubbed, ominous stains remained.

Suddenly Poirot uttered an exclamation. 'Those holes there – they are curious. One would say that they had been newly made.'

The holes in question were at the back of the chest against the wall. There were three or four of them. They were about a quarter of an inch in diameter and certainly had the effect of having been freshly made.

Poirot bent down to examine them, looking inquiringly at the valet.

'It's certainly curious, sir. I don't remember ever seeing those holes in the past, though maybe I wouldn't notice them.'

'It makes no matter,' said Poirot.

Closing the lid of the chest, he stepped back into the room until he was standing with his back against the window. Then he suddenly asked a question.

'Tell me,' he said. 'When you brought the cigarettes into your master that night, was there not something out of place in the room?'

Burgoyne hesitated for a minute, then with some slight reluctance he replied, 'It's odd your saying that, sir. Now you come to mention it, there was. That screen there that cuts off the draught from the bedroom door – it was moved a bit more to the left.'

'Like this?'

Poirot darted nimbly forward and pulled at the screen. It was a handsome affair of painted leather. It already slightly obscured the view of the chest, and as Poirot adjusted it, it hid the chest altogether.

'That's right, sir,' said the valet. 'It was like that.'

'And the next morning?'

'It was still like that. I remember. I moved it away and it was then I saw the stain. The carpet's gone to be cleaned, sir. That's why the boards are bare.'

Poirot nodded.

'I see,' he said. 'I thank you.'

He placed a crisp piece of paper in the valet's palm.

'Thank you, sir.'

'Poirot,' I said when we were out in the street, 'that point about the screen – is that a point helpful to Rich?'

'It is a further point against him,' said Poirot ruefully. 'The screen hid the chest from the room. It also hid the stain on the carpet. Sooner or later the blood was bound to soak through the wood and stain the carpet. The screen would prevent discovery for the moment. Yes – but there is something there that I do not understand. The valet, Hastings, the valet.'

'What about the valet? He seemed a most intelligent fellow.'

'As you say, most intelligent. Is it credible, then, that Major Rich failed to realize that the valet would certainly discover the body in the morning? Immediately after the deed he had no time for anything – granted. He shoves the body into the chest, pulls the screen in front of it and goes through the evening hoping for the best. But after the guests are gone? Surely, then is the time to dispose of the body.'

'Perhaps he hoped the valet wouldn't notice the stain?'

'That, *mon ami*, is absurd. A stained carpet is the first thing a good servant would be bound to notice.

And Major Rich, he goes to bed and snores there comfortably and does nothing at all about the matter. Very remarkable and interesting, that.'

'Curtiss might have seen the stains when he was changing the records the night before?' I suggested.

'That is unlikely. The screen would throw a deep shadow just there. No, but I begin to see. Yes, dimly I begin to see.'

'See what?' I asked eagerly.

'The possibilities, shall we say, of an alternative explanation. Our next visit may throw light on things.'

Our next visit was to the doctor who had examined the body. His evidence was a mere recapitulation of what he had already given at the inquest. Deceased had been stabbed to the heart with a long thin knife something like a stiletto. The knife had been left in the wound. Death had been instantaneous. The knife was the property of Major Rich and usually lay on his writing table. There were no fingerprints on it, the doctor understood. It had been either wiped or held in a handkerchief. As regards time, any time between seven and nine seemed indicated.

'He could not, for instance, have been killed after midnight?' asked Poirot.

'No. That I can say. Ten o'clock at the outside – but seven-thirty to eight seems clearly indicated.'

'There *is* a second hypothesis possible,' Poirot said

227

when we were back home. 'I wonder if you see it, Hastings. To me it is very plain, and I only need one point to clear up the matter for good and all.'

'It's no good,' I said. 'I'm not there.'

'But make an effort, Hastings. Make an effort.'

'Very well,' I said. 'At seven-forty Clayton is alive and well. The last person to see him alive is Rich –'

'So we assume.'

'Well, isn't it so?'

'You forget, *mon ami*, that Major Rich denies that. He states explicitly that Clayton had gone when he came in.'

'But the valet says that he would have heard Clayton leave because of the bang of the door. And also, if Clayton had left, when did he return? He couldn't have returned after midnight because the doctor says positively that he was dead at least two hours before that. That only leaves one alternative.'

'Yes, *mon ami*?' said Poirot.

'That in the five minutes Clayton was alone in the sitting-room, someone else came in and killed him. But there we have the same objection. Only someone with a key could come in without the valet's knowing, and in the same way the murderer on leaving would have had to bang the door, and that again the valet would have heard.'

'Exactly,' said Poirot. 'And therefore –'

'And therefore – nothing,' I said. 'I can see no other solution.'

'It is a pity,' murmured Poirot. 'And it is really so exceedingly simple – as the clear blue eyes of Madame Clayton.'

'You really believe –'

'I believe nothing – until I have got proof. One little proof will convince me.'

He took up the telephone and called Japp at Scotland Yard.

Twenty minutes later we were standing before a little heap of assorted objects laid out on a table. They were the contents of the dead man's pockets.

There was a handkerchief, a handful of loose change, a pocketbook containing three pounds ten shillings, a couple of bills and a worn snap-shot of Marguerita Clayton. There was also a pocketknife, a gold pencil and a cumbersome wooden tool.

It was on this latter that Poirot swooped. He unscrewed it and several small blades fell out.

'You see, Hastings, a gimlet and all the rest of it. Ah! it would be a matter of a very few minutes to bore a few holes in the chest with this.'

'Those holes we saw?'

'Precisely.'

'You mean it was Clayton who bored them himself?'

'*Mais, oui – mais, oui!* What did they suggest to you,

those holes? They were not to *see* through, because they were at the back of the chest. What were they for, then? Clearly for air? But you do not make air holes for a dead body, so clearly they were *not* made by the murderer. They suggest one thing – and one thing only – that a man was going to *hide* in that chest. And at once, on that hypothesis, things become intelligible. Mr Clayton is jealous of his wife and Rich. He plays the old, old trick of pretending to go away. He watches Rich go out, then he gains admission, is left alone to write a note, quickly bores those holes and hides inside the chest. His wife is coming there that night. Possibly Rich will put the others off, possibly she will remain after the others have gone, or pretend to go and return. Whatever it is, Clayton will *know*. Anything is preferable to the ghastly torment of suspicion he is enduring.'

'Then you mean that Rich killed him *after* the others had gone? But the doctor said that was impossible.'

'Exactly. So you see, Hastings, he must have been killed *during* the evening.'

'But everyone was in the room!'

'Precisely,' said Poirot gravely. 'You see the beauty of that? "Everyone was in the room." What an alibi! What *sang-froid* – what nerve – what audacity!'

'I still don't understand.'

'Who went behind that screen to wind up the phonograph and change the records? The phonograph and the chest were side by side, remember. The others are dancing – the phonograph is playing. And the man who does not dance lifts the lid of the chest and thrusts the knife he has just slipped into his sleeve deep into the body of the man who was hiding there.'

'Impossible! The man would cry out.'

'Not if he were drugged first?'

'Drugged?'

'Yes. Who did Clayton have a drink with at seven-thirty? Ah! Now you see. Curtiss! Curtiss has inflamed Clayton's mind with suspicions against his wife and Rich. Curtiss suggests this plan – the visit to Scotland, the concealment in the chest, the final touch of moving the screen. Not so that Clayton can raise the lid a little and get relief – no, so that he, Curtiss, can raise that lid unobserved. The plan is Curtiss's, and observe the beauty of it, Hastings. If Rich had observed the screen was out of place and moved it back – well, no harm is done. He can make another plan. Clayton hides in the chest, the mild narcotic that Curtiss had administered takes effect. He sinks into unconsciousness. Curtiss lifts up the lid and strikes – and the phonograph goes on playing "Walking My Baby Back Home".'

I found my voice. 'Why? But why?'

Poirot shrugged his shoulders.

'Why did a man shoot himself? Why did two Italians fight a duel? Curtiss is of a dark passionate temperament. He wanted Marguerita Clayton. With her husband and Rich out of the way, she would, or so he thought, turn to him.'

He added musingly:

'These simple childlike women . . . they are very dangerous. But *mon Dieu!* what an artistic masterpiece! It goes to my heart to hang a man like that. I may be a genius myself, but I am capable of recognizing genius in other people. A perfect murder, *mon ami*. I, Hercule Poirot, say it to you. A perfect murder. *Épatant!*'

Afterword

'The Mystery of The Baghdad Chest', first published in the *Strand Magazine* in January 1932, is the original version of 'The Mystery of the Spanish Chest', a novella included in the collection *The Adventure of the Christmas Pudding* (1960). The novella is told in the third person and Hastings does not appear.

Hercule Poirot's debut was *The Mysterious Affair at Styles* (1920), written by Christie in response to a challenge from her sister while working in a poisons dispensary in Torquay. When Poirot died fifty-five years later in *Curtain* (1975), published shortly before Christie's own death, one mystery remained unsolved: his age. Though the original text of *Curtain* was written some thirty years earlier, subsequent events mean we must assume the published novel to take place in the early 1970s, shortly after what was to be his 'penultimate' case, *Elephants Can Remember* (1972) was published. In *Curtain*, Poirot seems to be at least in his mid- to late-eighties, which would mean that he was in his early thirties in *The Mysterious Affair at Styles*. This novel is set in 1917 and in it Poirot is described as a 'quaint dandified little man with a bad limp . . . as a detective his flair had been extraordinary, and he had achieved triumphs by unravelling some of the most baffling cases of the day.' Moreover, in the short story in which Poirot first appeared, 'The Adventure at the Victory Ball', collected in *Poirot's Early Cases* (1974), he is described as having been 'formerly chief of the Belgian force'. Given his 'bad limp', it is possible that Poirot retired through ill health although it did not constitute much of a handicap in his many later cases. However, in *Styles*, Inspector James Japp, who appears in many later novels, recalled how he and Poirot had worked together in 1904 – 'the Abercrombie forgery case' – when Poirot could only have been a teenager if he was in his eighties in *Curtain*!

In September 1975, the writer and critic H. R. F. Keating suggested a possible solution in a piece to mark the publication of *Curtain* – Poirot was in fact *117* years of age at his death, and Keating went on to suggest that there might be other skeletons in the detective's closet!

Perhaps the last word should go to Poirot's creator who, in an interview in 1948, commented prematurely that 'He lived for such a long time. I really ought to have got rid of him. But I was never given the opportunity to do so. My fans wouldn't let me.' This was only a few years after *Curtain* had been written but nearly thirty years before it was published.

While the Light Lasts

I

The Ford car bumped from rut to rut, and the hot African sun poured down unmercifully. On either side of the so-called road stretched an unbroken line of trees and scrub, rising and falling in gently undulating lines as far as the eye could reach, the colouring a soft, deep yellow-green, the whole effect languorous and strangely quiet. Few birds stirred the slumbering silence. Once a snake wriggled across the road in front of the car, escaping the driver's efforts at destruction with sinuous ease. Once a native stepped out from the bush, dignified and upright, behind him a woman with an infant bound closely to her broad back and a complete household equipment, including a frying pan, balanced magnificently on her head.

All these things George Crozier had not failed to point out to his wife, who had answered him with a monosyllabic lack of attention which irritated him.

'Thinking of that fellow,' he deduced wrathfully. It was thus that he was wont to allude in his own mind to Deirdre Crozier's first husband, killed in the first year of the War. Killed, too, in the campaign against German West Africa. Natural she should, perhaps – he stole a glance at her, her fairness, the pink and white smoothness of her cheek; the rounded lines of her figure – rather more rounded perhaps than they had been in those far-off days when she had passively permitted him to become engaged to her, and then, in that first emotional scare of war, had abruptly cast him aside and made a war wedding of it with that lean, sunburnt boy lover of hers, Tim Nugent.

Well, well, the fellow was dead – gallantly dead – and he, George Crozier, had married the girl he had always meant to marry. She was fond of him, too; how could she help it when he was ready to gratify her every wish and had the money to do it, too! He reflected with some complacency on his last gift to her, at Kimberley, where, owing to his friendship with some of the directors of De Beers, he had been able to purchase a diamond which, in the ordinary way, would not have been in the market, a stone not remarkable as to size, but of a very exquisite and rare shade, a peculiar deep amber, almost old gold, a diamond such as you might not find in a hundred years. And the look in her eyes when he gave it to her! Women were all the same about diamonds.

The necessity of holding on with both hands to prevent himself being jerked out brought George Crozier back to the realities. He cried out for perhaps the fourteenth time, with the pardonable irritation of a man who owns two Rolls-Royce cars and who has exercised his stud on the highways of civilization: 'Good Lord, what a car! What a road!' He went on angrily: 'Where the devil is this tobacco estate, anyway? It's over an hour since we left Bulawayo.'

'Lost in Rhodesia,' said Deirdre lightly between two involuntary leaps into the air.

But the coffee-coloured driver, appealed to, responded with the cheering news that their destination was just round the next bend of the road.

II

The manager of the estate, Mr Walters, was waiting on the stoep to receive them with the touch of deference due to George Crozier's prominence in Union Tobacco. He introduced his daughter-in-law, who shepherded Deirdre through the cool, dark inner hall to a bedroom beyond, where she could remove the veil with which she was always careful to shield her complexion when motoring. As she unfastened the pins in her usual leisurely, graceful fashion, Deirdre's eyes swept round the whitewashed ugliness of the bare room. No luxuries here, and Deirdre, who loved comfort as a cat loves cream, shivered a little. On the wall a text confronted her. 'What shall it profit a man if he gain the whole world and lose his own soul?' it demanded of all and sundry, and Deirdre, pleasantly conscious that the question had nothing to do with her, turned to accompany her shy and rather silent guide. She noted, but not in the least maliciously, the spreading hips and the unbecoming cheap cotton gown. And with a glow of quiet appreciation her eyes dropped to the exquisite, costly simplicity of her own French white linen. Beautiful clothes, especially when worn by herself, roused in her the joy of the artist.

The two men were waiting for her.

'It won't bore you to come round, too, Mrs Crozier?'

'Not at all. I've never been over a tobacco factory.'

They stepped out into the still Rhodesian afternoon.

'These are the seedlings here; we plant them out as required. You see –'

The manager's voice droned on, interpolated by her husband's sharp staccato questions – output, stamp duty, problems of coloured labour. She ceased to listen.

This was Rhodesia, this was the land Tim had loved, where he and she were to have gone together after the War was over. If he had not been killed! As always, the bitterness of revolt surged up in her at that thought.

Two short months – that was all they had had. Two months of happiness – if that mingled rapture and pain were happiness. Was love ever happiness? Did not a thousand tortures beset the lover's heart? She had lived intensely in that short space, but had she ever known the peace, the leisure, the quiet contentment of her present life? And for the first time she admitted, somewhat unwillingly, that perhaps all had been for the best.

'I wouldn't have liked living out here. I mightn't have been able to make Tim happy. I might have disappointed him. George loves me, and I'm very fond of him, and he's very, very good to me. Why, look at that diamond he bought me only the other day.' And, thinking of it, her eyelids dropped a little in pure pleasure.

'This is where we thread the leaves.' Walters led the way into a low, long shed. On the floor were vast heaps of green leaves, and white-clad black 'boys' squatted round them, picking and rejecting with deft fingers, sorting them into sizes, and stringing them by means of primitive needles on a long line of string. They worked with a cheerful leisureliness, jesting amongst themselves, and showing their white teeth as they laughed.

'Now, out here –'

They passed through the shed into the daylight

again, where the lines of leaves hung drying in the sun. Deirdre sniffed delicately at the faint, almost imperceptible fragrance that filled the air.

Walters led the way into other sheds where the tobacco, kissed by the sun into faint yellow discoloration, underwent its further treatment. Dark here, with the brown swinging masses above, ready to fall to powder at a rough touch. The fragrance was stronger, almost overpowering it seemed to Deirdre, and suddenly a sort of terror came upon her, a fear of she knew not what, that drove her from that menacing, scented obscurity out into the sunlight. Crozier noted her pallor.

'What's the matter, my dear, don't you feel well? The sun, perhaps. Better not come with us round the plantations? Eh?'

Walters was solicitous. Mrs Crozier had better go back to the house and rest. He called to a man a little distance away.

'Mr Arden – Mrs Crozier. Mrs Crozier's feeling a little done up with the heat, Arden. Just take her back to the house, will you?'

The momentary feeling of dizziness was passing. Deirdre walked by Arden's side. She had as yet hardly glanced at him.

'Deirdre!'

Her heart gave a leap, and then stood still. Only one person had ever spoken her name like that, with the faint stress on the first syllable that made of it a caress.

She turned and stared at the man by her side. He was burnt almost black by the sun, he walked with a limp, and on the cheek nearer hers was a long scar which altered his expression, but she knew him.

'Tim!'

For an eternity, it seemed to her, they gazed at each other, mute and trembling, and then, without knowing how or why, they were in each other's arms. Time rolled back for them. Then they drew apart again, and Deirdre, conscious as she put it of the idiocy of the question, said:

'Then you're not dead?'

'No, they must have mistaken another chap for me. I was badly knocked on the head, but I came to and managed to crawl into the bush. After that I don't know what happened for months and months, but a friendly tribe looked after me, and at last I got my proper wits again and managed to get back to civilization.' He paused. 'I found you'd been married six months.'

Deirdre cried out:

'Oh, Tim, understand, please understand! It was so awful, the loneliness – and the poverty. I didn't mind being poor with you, but when I was alone I hadn't the nerve to stand up against the sordidness of it all.'

'It's all right, Deirdre; I did understand. I know you

always have had a hankering after the flesh-pots. I took you from them once – but the second time, well – my nerve failed. I was pretty badly broken up, you see, could hardly walk without a crutch, and then there was this scar.'

She interrupted him passionately.

'Do you think I would have cared for that?'

'No, I know you wouldn't. I was a fool. Some women did mind, you know. I made up my mind I'd manage to get a glimpse of you. If you looked happy, if I thought you were contented to be with Crozier – why, then I'd remain dead. I did see you. You were just getting into a big car. You had on some lovely sable furs – things I'd never be able to give you if I worked my fingers to the bone – and – well – you seemed happy enough. I hadn't the same strength and courage, the same belief in myself, that I'd had before the War. All I could see was myself, broken and useless, barely able to earn enough to keep you – and you looked so beautiful, Deirdre, such a queen amongst women, so worthy to have furs and jewels and lovely clothes and all the hundred and one luxuries Crozier could give you. That – and – well, the pain – of seeing you together, decided me. Everyone believed me dead. I would stay dead.'

'The pain!' repeated Deirdre in a low voice.

'Well, damn it all, Deirdre, it hurt! It isn't that I blame you. I don't. But it hurt.'

They were both silent. Then Tim raised her face to his and kissed it with a new tenderness.

'But that's all over now, sweetheart. The only thing to decide is how we're going to break it to Crozier.'

'Oh!' She drew herself away abruptly. 'I hadn't thought –' She broke off as Crozier and the manager appeared round the angle of the path. With a swift turn of the head she whispered:

'Do nothing now. Leave it to me. I must prepare him. Where could I meet you tomorrow?'

Nugent reflected.

'I could come in to Bulawayo. How about the Café near the Standard Bank? At three o'clock it would be pretty empty.'

Deirdre gave a brief nod of assent before turning her back on him and joining the other two men. Tim Nugent looked after her with a faint frown. Something in her manner puzzled him.

III

Deirdre was very silent during the drive home. Sheltering behind the fiction of a 'touch of the sun', she deliberated on her course of action. How should she tell him? How would he take it? A strange lassitude seemed to possess her, and a growing desire to postpone the revelation as long as might be. Tomorrow would be soon enough. There would be plenty of time before three o'clock.

The hotel was uncomfortable. Their room was on the ground floor, looking out on to an inner court. Deirdre stood that evening sniffing the stale air and glancing distastefully at the tawdry furniture. Her mind flew to the easy luxury of Monkton Court amidst the Surrey pinewoods. When her maid left her at last, she went slowly to her jewel case. In the palm of her hand the golden diamond returned her stare.

With an almost violent gesture she returned it to the case and slammed down the lid. Tomorrow morning she would tell George.

She slept badly. It was stifling beneath the heavy folds of the mosquito netting. The throbbing darkness was punctuated by the ubiquitous *ping* she had learnt to dread. She awoke white and listless. Impossible to start a scene so early in the day!

She lay in the small, close room all the morning, resting. Lunchtime came upon her with a sense of shock. As they sat drinking coffee, George Crozier proposed a drive to the Matopos.

'Plenty of time if we start at once.'

Deirdre shook her head, pleading a headache, and she thought to herself: 'That settles it. I can't rush the thing. After all, what does a day more or less matter? I'll explain to Tim.'

She waved goodbye to Crozier as he rattled off in the battered Ford. Then, glancing at her watch, she walked slowly to the meeting place.

The Café was deserted at this hour. They sat down at a little table and ordered the inevitable tea that South Africa drinks at all hours of the day and night. Neither of them said a word till the waitress brought it and withdrew to her fastness behind some pink curtains. Then Deirdre looked up and started as she met the intense watchfulness in his eyes.

'Deirdre, have you told him?'

She shook her head, moistening her lips, seeking for words that would not come.

'Why not?'

'I haven't had a chance; there hasn't been time.'

Even to herself the words sounded halting and unconvincing.

'It's not that. There's something else. I suspected it yesterday. I'm sure of it today. Deirdre, what is it?'

She shook her head dumbly.

'There's some reason why you don't want to leave George Crozier, why you don't want to come back to me. What is it?'

It was true. As he said it she knew it, knew it with sudden scorching shame, but knew it beyond

247

any possibility of doubt. And still his eyes searched her.

'It isn't that you love him! You don't. But there's something.'

She thought: 'In another moment he'll see! Oh, God, don't let him!'

Suddenly his face whitened.

'Deirdre – is it – is it that there's going to be a – child?'

In a flash she saw the chance he offered her. A wonderful way! Slowly, almost without her own volition, she bowed her head.

She heard his quick breathing, then his voice, rather high and hard.

'That – alters things. I didn't know. We've got to find a different way out.' He leant across the table and caught both her hands in his. 'Deirdre, my darling, never think – never dream that you were in any way to blame. Whatever happens, remember that. I should have claimed you when I came back to England. I funked it, so it's up to me to do what I can to put things straight now. You see? Whatever happens, don't fret, darling. Nothing has been your fault.'

He lifted first one hand, then the other to his lips. Then she was alone, staring at the untasted tea. And, strangely enough, it was only one thing that she saw – a gaudily illuminated text hanging on a whitewashed wall. The words seemed to spring out from it and hurl themselves at her. 'What shall it profit a man –' She got up, paid for her tea and went out.

On his return George Crozier was met by a request that his wife might not be disturbed. Her headache, the maid said, was very bad.

It was nine o'clock the next morning when he entered her bedroom, his face rather grave. Deirdre was sitting up in bed. She looked white and haggard, but her eyes shone.

'George, I've got something to tell you, something rather terrible –'

He interrupted her brusquely.

'So you've heard. I was afraid it might upset you.'

'*Upset* me?'

'Yes. You talked to the poor young fellow that day.'

He saw her hand steal to her heart, her eyelids flicker, then she said in a low, quick voice that somehow frightened him:

'I've heard nothing. Tell me quickly.'

'I thought –'

'Tell me!'

'Out at that tobacco estate. Chap shot himself. Badly broken up in the War, nerves all to pieces, I suppose. There's no other reason to account for it.'

'He shot himself – in that dark shed where the

tobacco was hanging.' She spoke with certainty, her eyes like a sleep-walker's as she saw before her in the odorous darkness a figure lying there, revolver in hand.

'Why, to be sure; that's where you were taken queer yesterday. Odd thing, that!'

Deirdre did not answer. She saw another picture – a table with tea things on it, and a woman bowing her head in acceptance of a lie.

'Well, well, the War has a lot to answer for,' said Crozier, and stretched out his hand for a match, lighting his pipe with careful puffs.

His wife's cry startled him.

'Ah! don't, don't! I can't bear the smell!'

He stared at her in kindly astonishment.

'My dear girl, you mustn't be nervy. After all, you can't escape from the smell of tobacco. You'll meet it everywhere.'

'Yes, everywhere!' She smiled a slow, twisted smile, and murmured some words that he did not catch, words that she had chosen for the original obituary notice of Tim Nugent's death. 'While the light lasts I shall remember, and in the darkness I shall not forget.'

Her eyes widened as they followed the ascending spiral of smoke, and she repeated in a low, monotonous voice: 'Everywhere, everywhere.'

Afterword

'While the Light Lasts' was first published in the *Novel Magazine* in April 1924. To those familiar with the works of Sir Alfred Lord Tennyson, Arden's true identity will not have come as a surprise.

Tennyson was among Christie's favourite poets, together with Yeats and T. S. Eliot, and his *Enoch Arden* also inspired the Poirot novel *Taken at the Flood* (1948). The plot of 'While the Light Lasts' was later used to greater effect as part of *Giant's Bread* (1930), the first of her six novels written under the pseudonym of Mary Westmacott. Although of less interest to many than her detective fiction, the Westmacott novels are generally considered to provide a commentary of sorts on some of the events of Christie's own life, a sort of parallel autobiography. In any event, they gave Christie an important means of escape from the world of the detective story, much to the chagrin of her

Agatha Christie

publishers who were understandably less than keen on anything that distracted her from the business of writing detective stories. The most interesting of the six is the aptly titled *Unfinished Portrait* (1934), which Christie's second husband, the archaeologist Max Mallowan, described as being 'a blend of real people and events with imagination . . . more nearly than anywhere else a portrait of Agatha.'

Her own favourite was the third Westmacott novel, *Absent in the Spring* (1944), which she described in her autobiography as, 'the one book that has satisfied me completely . . . I wrote that book in three days flat.' She commented, 'It was written with integrity, with sincerity, it was written as I meant to write it, and that is the proudest joy an author can have.'

ALSO AVAILABLE
BY CHARLES OSBORNE

The Life and Crimes of Agatha Christie

Agatha Christie was the author of over 100 plays, short story collections and novels which have been translated into 103 languages; she is outsold only by the Bible and Shakespeare. Many have tried to copy her but none has succeeded. Attempts to capture her personality on paper, to discover her motivations or the reasons for her popularity, have usually failed. Charles Osborne, a lifelong student of Agatha Christie, has approached this most private of people above all through her books, and the result is a fascinating companion to her life and work.

This 'professional life' of Agatha Christie provides authoritative information on each book's provenance, on the work itself and on its contemporary critical reception set against the background of the major events in the author's life. Illustrated with many rare photographs, this comprehensive guide to the world of Agatha Christie has been fully updated to include details of all the publications, films and TV adaptations in the 25 years since her death.

ISBN: 0 00 257033 5 Hardback
ISBN: 0 00 653097 4 Paperback

ALSO BY AGATHA CHRISTIE

Witness for the Prosecution and Selected Plays

The first-ever publication in book form of *Witness for the Prosecution*, Christie's highly successful stage thriller which won the New York Drama Critics Circle Award for best foreign play, plus three of her classic mysteries.

Witness for the Prosecution
A stunning courtroom drama in which a scheming wife testifies against her husband in a shocking murder trial . . .

Towards Zero
A psychopathic murderer homes in on unsuspecting victims in a seaside house, perched high on a cliff . . .

Go Back For Murder
When the young feity Carla, orphaned at the tender age of five, discovers 16 years later that her mother was imprisoned for murdering her father, she determines to prove her dead mother's innocence . . .

Verdict
Passion, murder and love are the deadly ingredients which combine to make this one of Christie's more unusual thrillers, which she described as 'the best play I have written with the exception of *Witness for the Prosecution*.'

ISBN: 0 00 649045 X

ALSO BY AGATHA CHRISTIE

Come, Tell Me How You Live

Agatha Christie was already well known as a crime writer when she accompanied her husband, Max Mallowan, to Syria and Iraq in the 1930s. She took enormous interest in all his excavations, and when friends asked what her strange life was like, she decided to answer their questions in this delightful book.

First published in 1946, *Come, Tell Me How You Live* gives a charming picture of Agatha Christie herself, while also giving insight into some of her most popular novels, including *Murder in Mesopotamia* and *Appointment with Death*. It is, as Jacquetta Hawkes concludes in her introduction, 'a pure pleasure to read'.

'Perfectly delightful . . . colourful, lively and occasionally touching and thought-provoking.'
CHARLES OSBORNE, *Books & Bookmen*

'Good and enjoyable . . . she has a delightfully light touch.'
MARGHANITA LASKI, *Country Life*

ISBN: 0 00 653114 8